A WICKED ENCOUNTER

IVY COLLINS

1

EMILY

I've been waiting half a year to play this game, but all I can think about is the hot blond guy leaning back in the chair directly next to me.

It's been six months since our regular gaming group finished its two-year-long campaign. I had to retire Julianna, my half-elven fashionista transmuter. I'm not gonna lie, I had a sniffle in the car afterward.

Okay, the sniffling *might* have had something to do with the fact that our gamemaster Finn used the last session to romantically propose to my roommate Liv... but I was also really emotional about putting the last bookend on that character's story.

Thankfully, my roommate is basically the best. Liv's been stretching her own storytelling muscles in the last year, and she promised the whole group that she'd run something special for us at TowerCon this year—a game where we'd get to bring back our old characters for one last hurrah. Liv even told Finn he could jump in and play Keller, one of his non-player characters from the game.

So here we are, all settled around the table in a hotel lobby on the Saturday night of TowerCon, while Liv sets the scene for the game. Only, there's two more people at the table than I was expecting, and one of them is *painfully* distracting.

"I hope you guys don't mind," Liv says shyly. "I don't see Luke and Ginny very often, and I really wanted to run something for them while I was at the con. I figured they could just guest star, since we're playing tonight anyway?"

There's a chorus of enthusiastic agreement around the table. Finn already knows both Luke and Ginny, and Samson and Jim are some of the most welcoming players I know. I mumble my own *yeah, sure,* sneaking peeks at the two players that have joined the table.

I dimly remember Ginny from last year's convention. She's short and adorable, with rounded cheeks and blonde pixie hair, streaked with pink highlights. Poor Ginny's very first game of *Towers & Tyrants* had a bad player at the table, and I know Liv's been beating herself up for forever because she thinks she didn't handle things well enough as the gamemaster. Ginny seems to have really bounced back from that experience in the last year, though—she's fully enthused for this year's con, dressed up in a green druid's robe and wearing latex elf ears. The costume isn't professional quality, but she's cute as a button, so she really makes it work.

Luke is... not adorable. No, *adorable* is not a word I'd use to describe him. *Sexy,* maybe. *A really good bad idea waiting to happen,* for sure. He's a long, lean specimen of a man, with dirty blond hair that falls into his eyes. *Blue* eyes. I already know that, because I've been looking at him *way* too much. Luke isn't costumed at all—at least, not in the usual way. He's dressed nicely, with a black button-down and slacks and a black-and-gold vest. Liv has already assured me he's the nicest guy in the world, but there's a kind of devil-may-care smirk on his lips that already has me going.

I have a thing for bad boys. It's almost like a disease. I blame my mother's copy of the movie *Labyrinth*. Ever since I watched it, I've had confusing feelings for blond, villainous men in formal clothing. Add a little guyliner, and I'm basically instant putty.

Luke isn't wearing guyliner, but he's got the well-dressed bad boy thing down pat. "You're sure you're good with me playing a lawful evil character?" he asks Liv skeptically. He *does* have a friendly voice, for all that he looks wickedly delicious.

"I've already accounted for it!" Liv says cheerily. "You guys will have mutual goals. I believe your cleric's god still hates demons?"

"Oh, he *certainly* does," Luke agrees. "Demons are far too unpredictable. Berlisle prefers his wickedness a little more disciplined."

I can't believe what I'm hearing. We're going to have a cleric of Berlisle in the group? "You're playing a *devil*-worshipper?" I manage.

Luke shoots me a winning smile that makes me go weak in the knees. He reaches out to take my hand and pretends to brush his lips across the back. His breath ghosts over my skin, and I shiver. "Archbishop Devlin Carr," he says. "At your service. I assure you, all of the terrible stories you've heard about me are absolutely true."

Oh. Sweet baby Jesus.

Luke lets go of my hand without another thought, as though he *didn't* just inspire me to imagine those lips traveling up my arm, and on to... other places.

"Ginny will be playing Queen Isadora Ephram," Liv tells us. "I made her up a character sheet. She'll be joining you for your mission undercover. Everyone in the group but Devlin will know who she is, obviously."

Luke shoots Ginny an arched eyebrow. "And who brought *this* useless chickadee?" he jokes.

Ginny rolls her eyes and smacks him on the shoulder. "You be careful, wise-ass," she says. "If you mouth off like that to me in-character, I could have you thrown in a dungeon."

Apart from the unique *distraction* that Luke brings to the table, I'm actually getting a good feeling off these two. They're clearly comfortable enough with each other to add a little edge to their banter.

"Before I forget," our bard Jim notes from my other side, "anyone want a beer? Liv said we're allowed to drink at her game, as long as we accept the natural consequences of our *impaired decision-making*." He grins at that.

Our cleric of luck, Samson, grabs a beer from underneath the table. "I'm gonna need to be *very* drunk, if you're playing that lute during game," he mutters. Jim strums the actual, honest-to-god lute he bought last year for his bard's costume. He has no idea how to play it. It's *also* wildly out of tune. I groan and grab a beer for myself.

"Yes, please," Luke says next to me. His voice is low and amused. "I never turn down an opportunity to indulge my vices."

I can't help squirming just a little bit at that. I'd love to indulge *his* vices.

Ahem.

I pass a beer over in his direction, and Liv begins setting the scene for us.

LUKE

God, I wish I was evil sometimes.

Ginny likes to make fun of me; she says I play evil characters so much because I'm secretly lawful good and kind of miserable about it. Frankly, she's not so far off the mark.

Right now, for example. I'm sitting next to the most stunning woman at this convention, wishing I cared less about the game I've been invited to and the feelings of its gamemaster. If I was less of a total sap, maybe I'd be openly hitting on the frankly gorgeous woman next to me, instead of consciously avoiding any hint of impropriety. I've seen what happens when guys corner a female player at the gaming table, and it's just not pretty.

But holy hell, does it *hurt* to be good. Emily is actually dressed up as her character—and I don't mean that in the casual sense. She's a professional cosplayer with her own online channel, which I *might* watch religiously. She's wearing a slim, peacock-colored dress that hugs her curves, slitted *very* high up on her legs to display those thigh-high leather boots of hers. I know for a fact that the bodice she's wearing to force that hourglass shape makes it hard for her to breathe—especially when she's sitting down, like she currently is—because she laughed about it at length in one of her videos. Emily's wearing honest-to-god elf ears, carefully painted to match her own skin tone... but the long red hair that spills down her shoulders is the real deal.

I've got the sexiest geek in the entire state of Texas sitting next to me, and I'm forcing myself not to act like I'm wildly attracted to her.

Evil people do not have this problem, god damn it.

"Elsinore is stalling for time at the negotiating table," Liv tells us, "but she can only do it for so long." Our gamemaster is blissfully unaware of my mental anguish. "You've only got a few hours to figure out which emissary is actually a demon in disguise."

"We'll need to search their rooms," Ginny says imperiously, "starting with *this* room." She turns toward Finn, at the edge of the table. "You—thief. Burglary is your speciality, isn't it? You can open this lock?"

Finn makes a show of sighing heavily. "I don't think anyone has ever so understated my skills before," he says. "Yes. I can unlock a door, Your Ma—" He side-eyes my character and changes his words midstream. "You're *mad* if you think I can't," he corrects himself.

I snort at that. It's an unexpected pleasure getting to play at a table with Finn. I'm a little less star-struck by his presence these days, since we've spent the last year occasionally hanging out over drinks, but he's still a well-loved gamewriter for T&T. Finn happens to have written the *Infernal Villains* sourcebook, which I use... rather a lot.

"Well then," Ginny declares. "There's no time like the present. The Chief Diplomat can't keep those scoundrels busy forever. Archbishop, I presume you'll know signs of demonic rituals if you see them?"

I blink. *Right.* I'm the Archbishop. She's addressing *me*. I haven't gotten to play Devlin in far too long—he's too high-level for most games. "I'm not sure whether I should take that as a compliment or resent the implications," I observe. "But yes. I'm well-learned in the ways of demons... and how best to remove them from this plane of existence."

The other cleric of the group—I think the player's name was Samson—gives me a narrow-eyed gaze. He's built like a tank, so it's a little intimidating *out-of-character* as well. "Don't think I don't have my eye on you, you devilish bootlicker," he tells me.

I throw him my best, most charming smile. "Now, I'm fairly certain *that* was a compliment," I tell him. "It's all right—I'm used to people being wildly attracted to me. You don't need to be embarrassed."

Jim, the bard, reaches out to press a hand against Samson's chest. "*Don't* let the devil-worshipper wind you up," he warns. "You're just entertaining him."

Samson lets out a low growl and crosses his arms.

"Wildly attracted to you?" Emily asks. She wrinkles her nose at me. "In *those* robes? With *that* broach? Oh *lord,* no. You need to reassess your wardrobe, sweetheart."

Oof. I know that's just an in-character zing, but that *stings.* I shake my head in her direction. "I fail to understand why *she's* here," I observe to the group. "Did someone need a dress made?"

Emily's lips twitch with humor, though I've just insulted her character. We're both having fun with this exchange—and I've just slow-pitched her a chance to make me eat my words.

"Uhh..." Finn cringes from across the table, catching our attention again. "That's a one. I rolled a one." He shakes his head disbelievingly. "The Prince of Thieves is... *not* starting this session off with a bang."

"Aw," Liv says, with a sympathetic pat on his shoulder. "Here, switch dice with me for next time. My d20's been lucky all day."

"The lock is giving me some trouble," Finn tells us with a sigh. "We'll need to take a different tack—"

"I use *Disintegrate Matter* on the lock," Emily says. She leans back in her chair and crosses her legs one over the other, holding my eyes with a satisfied smirk.

Don't make the hot elf girl uncomfortable, don't make the hot elf girl uncomfortable, definitely do not flirt with the very hot elf.

I take a very long swallow of my beer to prevent myself from saying something naughty.

"Er... *well,*" Liv says, startled. "That would do it." She rolls a die behind her screen and nods. "Julianna chants a single word and points her finger at the lock. An acid green ray of energy slams into it. The lock collapses into dust... along with a pretty large chunk of the door."

Emily's still holding my eyes. "*That's* why I'm here, baby," she purrs at me. "Any other questions?"

Yes. None of them suitable for public consumption.

"...huh," I mutter instead.

"Well, we *definitely* have to find some evidence now," Ginny sighs. "Otherwise we're going to have some difficulty explaining why half this diplomat's door is missing."

"Thankfully, that explanation would be Chief Diplomat Elsinore's job," Finn mutters to himself.

We spend the next hour or so investigating rooms, digging up all kinds of dirt and blackmail material in the process—some of which, my character quietly stashes away for a rainy day. The general atmosphere is pleasant; the banter is enjoyable. Before I know it, I'm three beers in, trying to prevent a thresher demon from murdering Ginny's borrowed royal character.

"Man, you know what we could *really* use right now?" Emily observes acidly. "Maybe a *paladin of Luin?*"

Liv grins at that. Her own player character, the paladin Elsinore, is obviously not appearing in this game, due to the fact that her player is *running* the game this time. "I'm afraid Elsinore is busy and cannot take your call right now," Liv says. "Leave a message after the beep, Julianna."

Emily purses her very red lips and finishes off the beer in her hand. "Okay, fine," she says. "Can you turn demons, Samson?"

"I can't," the cleric sighs. "I didn't take that ability."

"I *did* take that ability," I interject dimly. My brain is starting to slow down just a little bit from the alcohol. It's not enough to undo me, but I definitely feel a little bit silly for having forgotten such a basic aspect of my character. "That's not a bad idea. I'll turn back the demon."

"Ooh," Emily giggles. "The devil-worshipper is out-clericing you, Samson. You gonna let him do that?"

Samson snorts. "If you really feel that way, then maybe the *devil-worshipper* can take care of healing you from now on, Julianna."

"Maybe he can," Emily mutters under her breath. "Do clerics lay hands, or is that just paladins?"

I suck in a breath at that. *Don't hit on the hot elf girl,* I remind myself. It's not working. The hot elf girl is *flirting* now. That's like a green light, isn't it? I'm allowed to hit on her a *little* bit after that, right? "I am *excellent* at laying hands," I assure her. "I know a number of very lovely ladies who would be happy to act as a reference on my behalf."

Emily's very red lips part at that, and she lets out a soft noise. Her eyes are dilated, but I can't tell whether it's the alcohol or the flirting.

She uncrosses her legs. Crosses them again. Licks her lips.

Yeah, I'm pretty sure it's the flirting.

"Luke?" Liv interrupts my thoughts. "What's your roll?"

I blink and force my attention back to the game. "*Right*," I manage. "One second." I toss my d20 hurriedly, calculating up the total. "That's a turn-check of twenty-eight. I think."

"You think?" Liv sounds amused now.

"Your cleric of Berlisle could probably use a water or two to work off this alcohol," I admit. "Yes, definitely twenty-eight."

"You've made the roll with room to spare," Liv tells me. "Your unholy symbol flares with hellfire. The thresher demon cringes back, hissing at you... but it can't do much other than cower in the corner."

I nod slowly. "I think I'll ask it about its master. The rest of you might want to... step outside for a second. This could get unseemly."

"We're not going to let you torture that thing," Samson warns me.

"*That thing* is a demon with four bladed tails and a predilection for flaying its enemies alive," I tell him dryly. "You're not seriously going to tell me it deserves better?"

Samson hesitates uncertainly.

Finn considers this with a frown. "I don't think it deserves better," he says to me. "But *we* ought to be better than that."

"Says the Prince of Thieves?" I ask him wryly.

"Yes," Finn nods. "There was a time I'd have agreed with you, Devlin. But I've got to face Elsinore after this. I wouldn't be thrilled to tell her I let you torture some creature for information—not even a demon."

"Dame Elsinore strikes again," I sigh theatrically. "She's not even here, and she's still the bane of my existence." I wave a hand. "Fine. Kill it, then. We'll keep searching for proof."

The game hurtles onward. Soon enough, we do indeed have our proof of demon-dabbling. Ginny has the chance to dazzle me with the revelation that she's actually the queen herself. I'm really impressed with how much work Liv has put into the game as a whole.

I'm also desperately distracted by the fact that Emily has migrated to the hotel couch next to me. Somewhere in the middle of game, she peeled off those thigh-high boots and draped her bare legs across my lap.

"I guess... that's a wrap!" Liv says finally. She looks quite pleased with herself as she gathers up her dice. "I hope you guys had fun?"

"*Lots* of fun," I assure her. Liv beams at the compliment. Gamemasters are a bit light on the ground at the best of times, and I'm a habitual player. I consider it my solemn duty to shower my gamemasters with praise and keep them in the pool. "I hope Devlin wasn't too over-the-top for you," I add.

"Aw, no," Liv says with a smile. "It was fun trying to

run a bunch of different alignments at the table. You guys all played great off each other." She pushes up to her feet, collecting up her bag—but Finn grabs it from her before she can protest, slinging it over his shoulder and pecking her on the lips. It's so adorable, it's almost disgusting.

"Great job," Finn mumbles. "I had a blast."

Emily leans back into the arm of the couch. "Oh, get a room, you two," she laughs. She's... probably not one to talk. The bare skin of her ankle has just brushed my hand.

"We *have* a room," Finn says humorously. "And I think we'll go use it. I'm actually exhausted, and I've got games to run first thing in the morning."

Emily grins lazily, but she doesn't respond again.

"You coming back to the room, Emily?" Jim asks, as he and Samson start packing up their own stuff.

Emily purses her lips consideringly. "I think I'll hang out a little longer," she says. I'm almost positive that's supposed to translate to *I've got another room in mind.* Ginny, god bless her, has pulled out her car keys.

"I think I'll head on home," Ginny says, with an arched eyebrow in my direction. "I'd like to sleep in my own bed."

If I have indeed got lawful good in me, it's rearing its ugly, do-gooder head right now. I close my eyes and suck in a breath. "You shouldn't drink and drive," I tell Ginny. "You can still use the couch in the suite if you want."

Ginny snorts. "I had a ginger ale, Luke. I'm fine. It's *your* hotel room, so go use it."

You're a good woman, Ginny, I think, as I open my eyes again. I try very hard to beam this thought telepathically into her mind. I might even succeed, based on the smirk she gives me.

The rest of the group filters out of the hotel lobby. I'm left with a bare-legged, redheaded elf in my lap. Her foot nudges my hand. I rub at it absently, and she leans her head back into the couch arm, letting out a soft moan of approval.

"God, that's good," she murmurs. "I love this costume, but the boots just *kill* me."

This. This is the best convention ever.

Emily smiles at me from underneath her long, dark eyelashes. "You mind if I hang out in your room for a bit?" she asks.

As though I'm going to say no to *that*.

"You can hang out in my room as long as you want," I reply hoarsely.

Her smile turns sultry. "Great. Just let me grab my boots."

2

———

LUKE

"I don't guess you've ever seen the movie *Labyrinth?*" Emily mumbles, as we stumble through the door to my hotel room.

"Uh... is it a bad thing if I say no?" I ask warily.

Emily laughs. "Nooo. No, it's fine. Forget I said anything. It's just a thing." She shoots me a dizzy sort of grin. "Hey, this thing is really tight. I don't guess you could help me get it off?"

It takes me a second to realize she's talking about her bodice, specifically. My mouth goes dry. "Yeah," I say. "Yep, I could help you with that."

Devlin, I think, would be a hell of a lot smoother than this. Yet another reason I often wish I was more like my characters.

Emily lifts up her hair and turns around, pulling my hand toward the knot at the middle of her bodice. I have to work to undo the laces there, and not just because I'm a little tipsy. *Damn,* she's tied up tight.

She lets out another low moan of relief as the bodice

loosens, and I am literally in *pain.* I have never been so turned on before in my life.

The bodice slides down to the floor. Emily's only wearing that peacock-colored slip of a dress now; it drapes against her hard nipples, leaving very little to the imagination. She turns to plant both hands on my chest with another sultry smile and shoves me back into the hotel room chair. Now she's clambered up into my lap, straddling me directly, and I've got zero illusions left as to where this night is headed.

Emily's mouth closes on mine, hot and demanding. Her tongue slides between my lips, already eager. I think she's grabbed hold of my tie. What the hell kind of fantasy world am I living in?

I close my fingers around her bare thighs, sliding my hands up under the dress. Her hips are bare beneath the material and *oh god*, she's not wearing any underwear.

Right, I remember distantly. *This costume can't handle underwear lines.*

My hands close around her bare bottom, and Emily makes a high, desperate sound in the back of her throat, gripping my tie harder in her hands. All the blood has officially left my head to travel south, and I'm suddenly finding it a little hard to think.

Emily sways in my grip, and has to let go of my tie to catch herself against the chair. Her forehead presses into my shoulder, and a foreboding feeling at the bottom of my stomach curls up through the lust to instantly spoil the mood.

Oh come on. No. Please no. Leave me alone, conscience, this is such *a bad time.*

Emily's eyes are glazed as she looks up at me, and I'm

pretty sure a good portion of it is from the booze. "Mm," she mumbles. "I'm fine. Just gimme a second."

I've still got my hands on her bare ass. Her breasts are heaving in a *very* attractive manner. I've got the taste of some sugar-vanilla gloss on my lips. I know know *know* she's wet and willing beneath that tissue-thin dress.

I move my hands back up over the material of Emily's dress, smoothing it down over her legs.

Is this the best convention ever, or the worst convention ever? I can't tell anymore.

"You're, um... a little tipsy," I manage politely. *A little tipsy* is an understatement. I'm not even a hundred percent sure she remembers my real name right now. This is a huge mistake in the making, and I'm just sober enough to see it.

"Psh," Emily laughs. "Yeah." She nibbles at my neck, and I close my eyes against the feeling of her hot mouth on my skin. "I'm also *very* turned on."

No one would blame me, I try to convince myself. But this is quickly followed up with the glum thought: *I would blame me.*

Ugh. I really *am* some kind of self-torturing lawful good sap. God, I hate when Ginny's right.

"Hey," I mumble desperately. "Let's just... take a second. You're a little off-balance."

Emily pauses in the middle of nibbling my neck. "Don't need balance if I'm hora—horaz—" She stumbles over the word. "—*horizontal.*"

God damn it.

I settle my hands back under her thighs—but this time, it's to lift her up against me and carry her over toward the hotel bed. Emily moans dimly. It should be attractive, but it's too muddled and confused. I let her down onto the covers and slowly pry myself free from her grip.

"I'm just gonna grab a water," I tell her carefully. "We'll, uh... chat for a bit."

This is *not* what Emily wants to hear. But as she tries (and fails) to crawl back into an upright position, I'm even more depressingly certain than ever that it's the right thing to do.

I grab a water from the mini-bar and pull out my phone to text Finn.

LUKE: Emily's just this side of pass-out drunk. Can you ask Olivia to come and get her, just so she's okay for the night?

I set the phone surreptitiously aside and offer out the water to Emily. She blinks dazedly at me, and I go the extra mile, pulling off the cap for her.

Slowly, it begins to penetrate her alcohol-addled mind that I'm not about to get *horizontal* with her. Emily blinks quickly, and *oh no*, it's that level of drunk now, because over-the-top tears are gathering in her eyes.

"You, um. You. Don't want me?" Emily mumbles.

"I promise, I am *painfully* attracted to you," I mutter back. "Come on, let's hydrate you a bit."

Emily sniffles. She takes the water, but doesn't drink. "I'm pretty enough," she slurs. "So it's. It's the ears, isn't it? You're racist against *elves*." She tries to poke an accusatory finger into my chest, but she misses by a mile. I have to catch her to keep her from tumbling off the bed.

She's still warm and perfect, but my brain has finally switched fully over into seeing her as she is—drunk and vulnerable, and probably not firing on all cylinders.

"I am just as attracted to hot elven women as the next gamer," I tell her dryly. "*Please* have some water?" I shift her back onto the bed and pull the bottle back up toward her lips, as though to demonstrate.

Emily finally has a few swallows, thankfully. Some of the cold water misses the mark and trickles down to plaster her dress to her breasts. I drag my eyes back up quickly. *Drunk and vulnerable,* I remind myself.

God *damn* it, why hasn't Finn texted back?

"I'm..." *Hic.* "...so pathetic." Emily crumples against my chest, and now I'm *sure* she's a sad drunk. "Every... everyone in my gaming group is married now. 'Cept me. I can't even get a guy to *sleep* with me."

"Uh... Finn and Liv aren't married yet," I point out. "They're just engaged."

"I'm pretty sure you're not gettin' *engaged* to me!" Emily slurs. "I can't even get you to sleep with me!"

I could be tired, frustrated, or amused at this point. I choose *amused*, because it's the nicest alternative, and because frankly, this is just a *little* hilarious. Thankfully, I spent most of my college career as a designated driver, so none of this is new to me.

"I tell you what," I inform her seriously. "If you want to get engaged once you're sober, we'll have a serious adult conversation on the matter."

"What?" Emily blinks slowly. Her eyes are a pretty, clear-green color, even if they're a bit unfocused right now.

"You'd probably need to learn my name first," I add. I can't help the grin that steals over my face.

Emily narrows her eyes. "I know your name," she says.

I wait patiently.

"...Devlin." She frowns. "Wait. That's not right."

"You *definitely* shouldn't get engaged to *him*," I advise her.

Emily's nose wrinkles at that, and it's... kind of adorable, in spite of everything. "I'm not gettin' engaged at all," she sighs. "I can't even get a guy to sleep with me..."

Oh no. We're into the *endless drunken repetition* phase.

I take a swig of cold water and sigh. This is gonna be a long night.

EMILY

I'm in an unfamiliar hotel room, with a man's arm thrown across my waist and the mother of all hangovers.

My eyes are raw, and I think I've been crying—but it's hard to tell, since it could just be the hangover. My first thought is that I just spent most of last night crying all over poor Jim—but the guy behind me is wearing a very distinctive, un-Jim-like cologne, and there's no wedding band on his left hand.

Bits of last night come back to me in a blur, and I barely manage to suppress a moan of embarrassment.

I'm still fully-dressed—or at least, as close to fully-dressed as this costume gets. I shift to look behind me and wince. Luke—*yes*, his name is Luke, oh my god, not *Devlin*—hasn't even taken off his shoes, although I apparently got far enough to loosen his tie.

Even miserably hungover, I can appreciate the pure aesthetic appeal of the man behind me. That sandy blond hair falls into his eyes just *so*, and he's got a delicious-looking five o' clock shadow on his jaw now. If I wasn't nauseous and humiliated, I'd be *thrilled* to wake up next to this fantastic male specimen.

I'm just trying to decide how to extract myself from this miserable situation when a hard knock sounds at the door to the hotel room.

Luke blinks awake and catches me staring at him. I widen my eyes and scramble away like I've been burned.

"Em?" It's Olivia's voice on the other side of the door. She sounds concerned. "Hello, you there?"

Luke blinks a few times and sits up to rub at his face. "Ah," he yawns at me. "Morning." He pushes up to his feet and heads for the door. As he opens it, I lift my knees to my chest and bury my face into them, wishing that the bed would swallow me up and make me disappear forever.

"Em—oh! Hey, Luke." Liv sounds worried and just a little bit wary. "Is, um... is Em still here?"

Luke yawns again. "She's here," he says. "More-or-less in one piece. Probably super hungover. You got any Advil on you?"

Somehow, Luke doesn't sound either angry *or* miserable. Then again, we're both roleplayers. If anyone can put on a polite act, it's probably someone who pretends to be a devil-worshipper for five hours at a time.

"I'm pretty sure we've got some pain meds in the emergency kit in the T&T room at the con," Liv mumbles. She lowers her voice, but I still hear the next words. "I am... *so* sorry. Finn and I were both running games all day yesterday, we just slept like rocks as soon as we got back..."

Fantastic. My roommate's apologizing for me now. I

mean, I don't blame her in the *least*, but there's just a special sort of awful that comes with hearing sweet little Liv get embarrassed over my behavior.

"No problem," Luke says, though I'm pretty sure it was a *big* problem. "We handled it. Everything's cool."

I take a deep breath and try to ignore the ringing in my brain. I'm a fully-grown adult in fake elf ears, and it's time to face the music. I uncurl myself and stumble to my feet, snatching up my boots from the floor.

Does it count as a walk of shame if nothing actually *happened?*

Liv blinks at me as I slink toward the door, and I wince. Yep. This is still a special kind of shame.

"You look *awful,*" Liv says in a bewildered voice.

I shoot her a dark look. "I'm trying out a new cosplay," I say. "I call it *hungover con-goer.* Maybe I'll put it on my channel for posterity."

Luke coughs on a laugh. I feel a tiny bit better at that.

I hug my boots to my chest and tiptoe out the door next to Olivia. "I am... *so* sorry," I mumble at Luke, in the smallest voice I've ever used. I can't bring myself to look at him as I pass.

Luke shrugs awkwardly. "I've handled worse," he assures me. "At least you're not a fighty drunk. I once had a buddy give me a black eye and *then* throw up all over me."

I close my eyes. *At least you didn't give me a black eye* is not the most comforting comparison ever. "Right. Um."

Liv is looking at me with a sympathetic half-smile as I open my eyes again. She puts her arm around my shoulders. "Hey. Let's... get you some painkillers. We'll get you back to your hotel room and get you a shower."

As we head off, she mouths a *thank you* over my shoulder at Luke, and I pretend not to see it.

"You doing okay?" Liv asks me carefully, once we're well out of earshot.

I stare hollowly ahead. "I'm not a hundred percent sure," I say. "But I might have asked that poor man to marry me last night."

Liv presses a hand over her mouth. At first, I think she's covering an expression of horror—but then, a trickle of helpless laughter slips out, and I sigh heavily.

"Oh my god, I'm so sorry," Liv manages. "I shouldn't laugh."

"No," I say glumly. "No, it's funny, Liv. I'd laugh too, if I wasn't so godawful embarrassed."

Liv gives a tiny snort in between giggles. "Did... did he say yes?"

I press my fingers into my forehead. "*Please* don't tell Finn," I beg her. "Or Jim. Or Samson. Or... actually, just please don't tell anyone."

Liv takes a shaky breath, trying to get her laughter under control. "I am sworn to roommate secrecy," she assures me. Then: "Um. Just so I know. You didn't actually...?"

I press my lips together. "No," I say, to the unspoken question. "Nothing happened. I'm pretty sure I've *fully* wrecked that possibility."

Liv squeezes my shoulders. "I'm sorry," she says. "You want me to skip out on my games today and veg with you? We have some alternate gamemasters who could step in."

I shake my head. "No, no," I mumble. "I'll just feel

even more stupid that way. Let me marinate alone in my shame for a day or two."

Liv drops me off at the hotel room I've been sharing with Jim and Samson and takes off for the games she's supposed to be running. I pry off my elf ears and climb into the shower. The hot water washes off most of my makeup, but I'm pretty sure *nothing* will ever wash off this feeling of crippling embarrassment.

3

———

LUKE

I'm tired enough that I'd probably sleep through Sunday morning if it was my decision. But I promised Ginny we'd play board games, so I grab a quick shower and drag myself down to meet her in the board game room.

When I see her, she's *painfully* chipper and raring to go. "Sheep-collecting time!" Ginny declares with a grin. "Remember, we agreed to go cut-throat today. No truces, no holding back—we get drinks afterward and bury the hatchet."

I yawn broadly. "How about we get ginger ales and bury the hatchet?" I ask. "I think I'm good on booze for a while."

Ginny raises both her eyebrows at that. "That's funny," she says. "I figured you'd be in a great mood today." She doesn't come out and *ask* about my implied sleepover, because Ginny is classy like that.

I rub at my jaw. "Uh... plans went sideways," I admit tiredly. "We'll leave it at that."

Ginny winces. "Eesh. Uh... *how* sideways?" she asks delicately. I know then that I probably look like more of a wreck than I figured.

"I would hate to embarrass anyone," I mumble. "You know the bro code. You can keep a secret, right?"

Ginny snorts. "I'm pretty sure the bro code is all about kissing and telling," she says, as we grab a board game and settle into a free table. "But I know *your* bro code, yeah. I'll keep my lips sealed."

I still hesitate a bit. But I've got to tell *someone*, and I feel a hell of a lot more comfortable telling Ginny than any of the other people in my life. "The lady in question was *very* drunk," I sigh. "I had to talk her down and put her to bed."

Ginny cringes. "*Oh,*" she says. "That's... awkward."

"*So* awkward," I mutter. I grab a player token and a starting hand of resource cards. "Are we good friends, Ginny?" I ask her. "Am I allowed to complain at you about sex?"

Ginny bursts out laughing. "You're not my type, Luke," she assures me. "I don't have any secret crushes on you. Go ahead."

"Ouch," I say dryly. But I roll the dice and keep talking anyway. "I've watched Emily's cosplay channel for the last two years. I'm not even *into* cosplay. She's just... hot and geeky, and she does things with latex that make me uncomfortable." I rub at my face. "I had my dream woman throwing herself at me all night, and I had to say no. I'm not saying I should have done anything different... but it was *miserable*. And I'm pretty positive there's not gonna be a repeat performance."

Ginny shakes her head. "That's rough," she agrees.

"Man, we've gotta find you a nice gamer girl. Why *aren't* you dating anyone? Weren't you going out with some girl from your Nordic LARP?"

I groan. "Lacy, yeah. She moved to *Alaska.* I got the *it's not you, it's my career* talk."

Ginny nods sagely. "It's not you," she agrees. "Lacy just needed more caribou in her life, clearly." Ginny rolls the dice and pauses. "Speaking of four-legged creatures —can you pass me two more sheep?"

I pluck two sheep from the library and shove them over toward her.

"I'm trading four sheep for one brick of clay," Ginny informs me, sliding over the cards. "I'm gonna build me a whole road out of sheep," she adds under her breath. She looks up and raises an eyebrow at me. "So, let me get this straight. You're unattached, you lawful good-ed yourself out of your dream woman, and you have zero plans to go for round two with her?"

I blink. "Gin," I say. "She's *humiliated.* I'm pretty sure she's going to avoid me from now until doomsday."

Ginny grins. "Oh come *on,*" she says. "Dial it back to neutral good for just a *little* bit, would you? You have Finn's phone number. Emily's in his group. Are you seriously telling me you can't think of a reason to run into her again?"

I stare down wordlessly at my collection of clay and stone.

Ginny eyes me suspiciously. "You know what I think?" she says. "I think you're just worried you're gonna get shot down. And look—that's totally valid. But I *also* think you're gonna kick yourself forever if you don't give it one more try."

I scowl down at the dice. "I'm putting the bandit on your pastures," I tell her. "Gimme a goddamn sheep."

Ginny beams at me and offers out her hand. I steal one fluffy sheep and console myself with the brief sense of victory.

I am *not* a coward. I'm just being polite.

...I'm *pretty* sure I'm not a coward.

Fine. I'm a cowardly sheep-thief. But I'm pretty sure I'll manage to forget about this whole weekend, given just a year or two.

EMILY

I *do* feel a lot better, once I've had an herbal tea and a little more sleep. But I don't dare show my face at the con—the idea of running into Luke just *mortifies* me. I get on my channel's social media and fib about having caught the con crud, to explain why I'm not posting any more photos. The outpouring of little hearts and *get well soon*'s makes me feel simultaneously comforted and guilty.

Please, I think. *I'm not obliged to share my sex life with people. I'm allowed to take the diplomatic approach.*

It *does* bug me a little bit that I have to cop out of the day's photos. I make an okay side-income from my channel through subscriptions, but I probably could have put up a few sponsored posts today too. Oh well. Nothing like a little lost income to teach you not to drink too much.

Jim and Samson get back from the con a while later, and Samson shoots me a sympathetic look. "Con crud already?" he asks. I groan. *Obviously,* our entire gaming group follows my channel. They just like being supportive.

"Hangover," I correct him. It's not *entirely* a lie. "Are we heading home? I cannot *wait* to get out of here."

Samson nods. "I'll carry your stuff down to the car if you want," he offers.

I give him a piteously grateful look. "You can have the ring of advanced shielding next time we play," I tell him.

"Fancy," Samson grins. "You should get drunk more often." He hauls one of my not-insignificant makeup cases onto his shoulder and grabs his own rolling suitcase. "You mind checking us out, Jim?" he asks. "Just make sure Em stays in the room to let me in again. This'll be a few trips."

Jim pecks his husband on the lips. "I've got it covered," he assures Samson.

I throw a few things back into my suitcase as Samson goes back and forth to the car. I'm wearing some comfy sweats, and I don't intend to put on anything more dramatic.

I'm partway through folding up my gown for Julianna when a terrible realization hits me over the head.

"Em?" Jim asks curiously. "You okay? You look like you're about to hurl."

I sink my face into my hands. "My bodice," I mumble. "I left my bodice... somewhere else."

Jim blinks at me. "In the hotel?" he asks. "We could ask if someone found it and turned it in."

Yeah, I think glumly. *Maybe Luke left it with the front desk?* I could only be so lucky.

"Other hotel," I say. "But yeah. I'll run in and ask real quick before we leave."

I stop by the hotel across the street from us and ask the receptionist if anyone's turned in a bodice. She shakes her head, and my heart sinks. Did Luke even notice it in his room? Maybe he just overlooked it. I leave my phone number and ask them to call me if one of the cleaning crew finds it... but I don't expect to see it ever again.

Damn it. I *loved* that bodice. Then again, it's probably forever tainted by embarrassing memories now. Probably for the best, right?

"Did they find it?" Jim asks, as I slide into the back seat of the car.

I shake my head. "They'll call if it shows up," I mumble.

"Ugh, that's a shame," Samson sighs. "You put so many hours into that thing."

I shrug uncomfortably. "It's not the first time I've lost a costume piece," I say. "I'll get over it."

But by the time they drop me off at my apartment, I'm now feeling embarrassed *and* stupid.

4

LUKE

It's Monday morning, and I've got a huge problem sitting out on my kitchen table.

I found the satin, hand-embroidered bodice discarded on the other side of my hotel room chair while I was packing up to leave.

Leaving the thing with the hotel front desk struck me as too risky. I knew how long Emily had spent on it—hell, I watched the time lapse video.

The smart thing to do would be to call Finn and hand it over.

That would be the *smart* thing. Definitely the easy thing.

Maybe I'm feeling a little less lawful today... or maybe that conversation with Ginny is getting to me. I've got the perfect excuse to try and get past this awkwardness right in front of me. If I take the coward's way out and give the bodice to Finn, I can't pretend I'm just being polite. Because *surely*, Emily would be even more embarrassed to have her gamemaster hand it over, even if he already knew she'd been in my room.

I stare at the bodice a little longer than I should, given that I have to get into work soon. But eventually, I pull out my phone and navigate to the *Silverhart Cosplay* channel.

I know I'm close to losing my nerve, so I send the quickest DM in history before I can choke.

LUKE: Sorry to bother you here. I found one of your costume pieces. I can drop it off with you sometime this week?

The deed is done. I spend a while waiting, even though I know Emily probably doesn't check her social media messages during the work day. But eventually, I manage to close the tab and head to my car.

I've got number-crunching to do. It's the most boring, fully-absorbing thing in the world, so hopefully it'll keep my mind off my phone for a bit.

EMILY

Halfway through my shift on Monday morning, I put a pin in the wedding dress I'm working on—literally—and head to lunch. While I'm waiting on my sandwich, I check idly through my phone.

There's a message waiting for me on my *Silverhart* account. I have to read it three or four times, because my brain is too panicked to fully process it.

"Ohhh my god," I groan, pressing a hand over my eyes.

Somehow, Luke has found my channel. Honestly, that's not too crazy—I hand out business cards at the con like they're candy, and everyone in my group likes to brag on me. But that means Luke has read my lame cop-out about getting con crud yesterday, *and* he's probably seen a bunch of my self-serving pics where I show off my cleavage and kiss at the camera. That's never really bugged me before—real silk doesn't come cheap, and a girl's gotta eat—but it bugs me *now*. Literally every side he's seen of me so far is stupid and shallow and annoying. I know I've got better virtues, and it's not a crime to look sexy on the Internet... but god *damn* has this put me in a miserable frame of mind.

I spend all of lunch staring at the message, unable to think about anything else. I barely think to nibble at my sandwich. When I come back into the shop—*Sweet Threads*, for all your tailoring needs—my boss Andrea gives me a bewildered look.

"You look like someone stole your lunch money," she says. "What's up?"

I groan and throw myself into the chair next to the counter. "I don't even know where to begin," I mutter. But somehow, I manage to get through the whole embarrassing story anyway. I don't bother leaving out any details—Andrea's a mature adult, and she's told me worse stuff before.

Andrea purses her lips as I show her the message on my phone. "Sweetheart," she says gently, "I don't want to tell you your business, but I'm pretty sure you're overthinking things. Either he's the sort of nice guy who tracks down strange women to give them back their expensive stuff, or else he's still wildly interested."

I narrow my eyes at her. "I'm *never* attracted to nice guys," I say flatly. "You know that. It's my stupid—"

"—David Bowie villain thing," Andrea finishes for

me, bemused. "Yeah, I know. But there's got to be a first time for everything, huh?" She raises an eyebrow at me. "Your friends like him just fine. He dealt with a drunk woman all night long and didn't lose his temper. I'm not saying you *have* to go for it, but if I had a magic 8-ball in front of me, I bet all signs would point to yes."

I chew on my lip and glance down at my phone again.

There was a brief, shining moment on Saturday night where I thought I was going to bed with a hot, single gamer guy who *did things* to my libido. But that was Saturday, at a convention, and there are just different rules at a con. Rules like *you can have a one-night stand, and if it doesn't work out, you go your separate ways forever.* No contact info exchanged. No awkward apologizing that you're just not as into the relationship as the other person is.

"If I respond to this message," I say slowly, "I have to be a total adult about everything afterward. Like... what if there's a date? I don't even know anything about him, except that he looks good in a tie and he likes playing evil characters."

Andrea shrugs and hands me a pair of fabric shears. "I've said my piece. If you *don't* want my advice, giving it to you again won't change a thing." She raises an eyebrow at me. "Now, I've got a custom veil to finish. Come help me cut out the pattern."

I'm busy enough for the afternoon that I manage to distract myself from the message on my account. But when I get home and get back onto my social media to handle posting for the night, I can't help staring it down.

I start writing a response once or twice—but I erase it completely every time.

I let out a frustrated sigh and head out to knock on Liv's bedroom door. She stayed the night with Finn on Sunday, but I know she's back because I heard the front door close earlier.

"Come in!" Liv calls out.

I slink inside like I'm doing the walk of shame all over again, even though I know that's not the case. Liv gives me a curious look from behind her laptop.

"What do you know about Luke?" I blurt out.

Liv blinks. A little smile breaks out across her face before she can hide it, and I get the feeling she's about to proselytize the man to me like he's a religion.

"I met him at my first-ever tabletop game," Liv says. "He was *incredibly* nice. And he really came through during that incident last year at the con. I don't know a lot about what he does outside of gaming, but I'd trust him with just about anything at a gaming table."

I frown at Liv, searching for an excuse to contradict her. "So why does he always play evil characters?" I challenge her.

Liv shrugs. "He said something about working in customer service. I mean, I don't know what he gets out of it specifically, but he's never made anyone uncomfortable with it as far as I can tell."

Ergh. He's made *me* plenty uncomfortable with it, but more in a *that's uncomfortably sexy* sort of way. I decide not to bring that up. "But you really have no idea what he's like outside of the con?" I ask.

Liv purses her lips. "Not really," she admits. "I know he goes out for beers with Finn sometimes. They get along pretty well."

I sigh heavily. Nothing about this conversation is

giving me an excuse to ghost the man forever and safely forget this whole embarrassing experience.

"Okay," I mutter in a defeated voice.

"Okay?" Liv looks at me curiously. "Okay... what?"

I shoot her a frustrated glare. "Okay... he *might* have messaged me. And I'm going to be an adult and message him back." Liv suddenly looks like I've brought her an early Christmas gift, and I hurry to add: "He might just be giving me my bodice back. There's probably nothing date-worthy about it at all."

"You could always *make* it date-worthy," Liv suggests mischievously.

The very idea makes me nauseous again. I'm barely courageous enough to send this man back a message, let alone ask him out on a date. But I force myself to consider the possibility. "We'll see how brave I'm feeling," I say finally.

I head back to my room and chew on the message for a few more minutes, before finally typing a reply.

SILVERHART: Thanks. I appreciate it. I can meet you at Liv's coffee shop if you want?

I send the reply and settle in with a knot in my stomach. It's barely a minute before he responds.

LUKE: Tomorrow at seven?

Oh my god, I'm doing this. Why on earth am I doing this?

It's too late. I've gone too far.

SILVERHART: Sounds good. I'll see you then.

5

———

LUKE

J'm not a sports fan. But I know my sports metaphors, more-or-less, and I have a feeling we've just gone into overtime.

That *is* the right metaphor, isn't it? Whatever. In gamer terms, it was looking like a total party kill, but someone downed a healing potion at the last second and got back up for another round.

My point is, I'm pretty sure I've got exactly one shot at this, and I've got to make it count.

I head into *Cup o' Joe's* with a discreetly-wrapped bodice under my arm. Liv is working behind the counter —she looks over as I walk through the door and grins with badly-hidden delight. I'd be embarrassed, but it's probably a good sign that I've got the roommate in my corner.

I stop at the counter and decide to take a marginal risk. "Evening Elsie," I say. I've long since gotten into the habit of using Liv's character name—she's never corrected me, so I surely can't be bothered to correct *myself.* "Can I get an americano and one of whatever Emily's favorite drink is?"

Liv's smile widens. "Americano and a mocha," she says. "Coming right up." She leans in and whispers: "Em likes the brownies too."

I nod sagely. "A brownie too, then. You're a lady and a scholar, Dame Elsinore."

Liv beams at me. "Em's over at the table in the back," she tells me. "I'll bring everything out to you."

I head toward the back of the shop and find Emily sitting cross-legged in an oversized bean bag chair. It's a little weird not seeing her in a costume. She's dressed for the summer weather in a green tank top and jeans. Her red hair is back in a more practical ponytail, instead of carefully styled to fall over her shoulders just *so.* There are zero fake elf ears in sight.

Emily looks up at me as I approach and goes instantly beet red.

Yep, I confirm to myself. *Still wildly attracted to her.*

I offer out the bodice, and Emily snatches it from me. Her mortification is so obvious on her face that I can't help but feel bad. I clear my throat. "I'd ask if I can get you a coffee," I start apologetically, "but I'm afraid I already did."

Emily blinks quickly. "Um." The red flush on her face has yet to recede. "Thanks. I mean... for that, and for bringing this back." She pauses. "And for other things."

There is no dignified way to sit down in a bean bag chair, so I don't bother trying. I throw myself into the one across from her. "I'm not going to say it was a fun night," I admit. "But I like to think it's just common decency not to take advantage of a drunk person."

That color on her face doesn't disappear. Emily sinks back a little into her bean bag. "Common decency isn't always super common," she mutters. She hugs her bodice to her chest. "I just want you to know, I... I'm not like that normally. Like—I don't regularly get drunk and throw myself at guys, I *promise*."

I blink at that. "I didn't say you did," I reply carefully. "Not that it's any of my business, either way."

Emily sighs heavily. "You can stop being super nice about this whole thing at *any* point," she tells me. "Honestly, it'd probably make me feel a little more comfortable."

I grin at that. "Don't ask me to roleplay," I tell her. "I can get *very* mean when I roleplay."

Emily's fingers curl into her palms at that, and I swear I see her shiver. "Mm," she mumbles. "Uh. So noted."

Liv comes by with our drinks and sets a brownie in front of Emily, who stares at it as though it's an alien object. "What... what is this?" she asks.

"A brownie and a mocha," Liv informs her, with a bit of a triumphant smile. "You chocoholic."

Emily raises her eyebrows at me, and I take a sip of my americano. "If you're going to be humiliated, you may as well have some chocolate to soften the blow," I tell her.

Liv heads off, and Emily shakes her head at me disbelievingly. "Okay," she says finally. "What is *wrong* with you?"

I blink. "Uh... pardon?" I ask.

Emily leans forward, staring at me intently. "There's got to be *something*," she accuses me. "You're handsome, you're *nice*, and now you've bought me chocolate. I am never this lucky, so I'm sure there's something I ought to know."

I chew on that for a second. As flattering as all that is, I'm sure she's probably right. "Huh," I think aloud. "Well... okay. I've got an admission."

Emily straightens, waiting cautiously.

"I watch your channel," I tell her. "*Have* watched it, for about two years. I mean, not stalker-y watched it, but I can't say I didn't know you on sight."

Emily's eyes widen, and at first I worry that I've said the thing that's going to turn her off. But she bites at her lip. "You... like cosplay?" she asks hesitantly.

I'm sure the right answer to this question is *yes*—but that answer would also be a bit of a lie. I shake my head. "I like... *looking* at cosplay," I admit. "Like, I'm not an artist, and I don't want to be. But it's cool watching someone sculpt a statue."

Emily chews on this for a moment. "So... what *do* you do?" she asks. "Other than game. Liv said something about customer service."

I wince. "Oh, okay," I admit. "There's my dark secret." I clear my throat and lean forward, pitching my voice much lower. "I'm a CPA now. But I worked my way through college as a telemarketer. I'm pretty sure I murdered my first non-player character because my gamemaster made her sound too much like Karen-who-wants-to-talk-to-my-manager."

Emily goggles at me. Then, slowly, she begins to giggle. "Oh... my god," she manages. "Okay. That makes total sense."

I arch a skeptical eyebrow. "It does?"

Emily nods seriously. "Please," she says. "I can't hold

in-character stuff against people. I think I've hit on every halfway-handsome villain in the game—except for Keller, *obviously*, since it was clear he had the hots for Elsinore."

I consider that for a long moment. I can't help the twitch at the corner of my mouth. All right. Emily likes villains—*fictional* villains, of course. I'm suddenly a lot more confident in my plans to extend this short coffee meeting.

"Well," I say slowly. "Let me pitch something to you, then." Emily raises her eyebrows at me, and I continue. "I'm headed to a Nordic-style LARP two weekends from now. It's a once-a-year thing; we rent out a big bed-and-breakfast on a ranch and play for two days. It's a pretty dark game—but if you're interested in coming, I can beg you a last-minute character off the organizers."

Emily blinks slowly. "...Nordic LARP," she says slowly. "Like... live-action gaming, no hard rules?"

"*Consent* rules," I correct her. "There no randomness involved, partially because of the edgy stuff. Someone proposes an outcome, and everyone in the scene has to agree."

Emily licks her lips, and I can tell she's seriously considering the idea. "How edgy?" she asks. "Like, what's it about?"

"Modern-day sorcerers," I tell her. "Not everyone is evil, but some of the factions do things like blood sacrifice or demon-summoning. Basically, you can be as heroic or as villainous as you want." I pause. "I'm, uh. Clearly playing a blood sorcerer. But I can recommend you a more pleasant faction if you like."

Emily narrows her eyes. "Two weeks isn't a lot of time

to put together a costume," she muses. It's at that point that I know I've piqued her interest.

"I know this might be some kind of heresy," I tell her. "But if you haven't noticed, I barely costume, and no one cares. You can get away with a nice suit and some shades."

Emily scoffs. "Please," she says. "If I'm doing this, I'm at *least* repurposing some stuff from my closet." She smiles slowly. "Okay. I'm interested. But you said it's a bed-and-breakfast. Do I need to rent a room?"

I clear my throat a bit. This is probably the harder sell. "The rooms are all taken by now," I admit. "Technically, the characters are too, but the organizers owe me a definite favor or two by now. I don't mind letting you crash with me in my room. I'm happy to be a gentleman and take the couch."

Emily's quiet for a long moment—and at first, I worry this is the part that's scared her off. But she nods slowly. "Okay," she says. "*One* condition."

I raise an eyebrow. "We're on to the bargaining phase, I see."

Emily grins mischievously at me. "I want to do your makeup."

I blink at that. "Uh... makeup?"

Emily nods seriously. "If you're playing some evil sorcerer, you are *required* to wear guyliner," she tells me. "It's a rule, I didn't make it up."

I snort into my coffee. I can't say I've ever worn makeup before. But letting Silverhart put some guyliner on me seems like a relatively small price to pay for getting to shamelessly hit on her all game.

"Fine," I say. "But I get a condition too." I grin at her.

"This is a date. And I fully intend to seduce your character with my wicked ways." I pause. "Out-of-character seduction is absolutely optional, of course."

Emily presses her lips together. I'd wonder if she was offended, if I couldn't see her crossing and uncrossing her legs again. "Deal," she says quickly. "Send me the details. And let me know what kind of costume I need for my character, ASAP."

She taps her personal phone number into my phone, and I make a mental apology to Corinna, who runs the LARP every year. She's going to *kill* me when I ask for a last-minute character.

It's absolutely going to be worth it.

EMILY

I'm probably crazy. I've just agreed to go out in the middle of nowhere in Texas with a guy I barely know. *And* I'm going to sleep in his room.

"You'll be fine," Liv assures me that night, though I haven't mentioned the *one room* part to her. "We all know where you're going to be and who you'll be with. Plus, like... your thousands of social media followers. I can't imagine you won't be posting pics."

I sigh. "I'm actually not worried at all, is the weird part," I admit. "I guess... I've already been as stupid around him as it gets, and the only thing that got injured was my ego."

Liv beams at that. "So there you go," she says. "Make yourself a smoking hot costume and go enjoy yourself for a weekend."

I frown at my phone. "Okay, *that's* the part I'm

nervous about," I mutter. "I've got two weeks to figure out a costume, and I haven't even got my character yet. I've never worked on such a tight deadline."

Liv snorts. "Think of it as a challenge," she tells me. "Your fans will love it. It can be like... bringing back your greatest hits from the closet and remixing them."

I nod, but I'm skeptical. Liv knows what a perfectionist I am. I run a professional cosplay channel. If I'm not the best-dressed person at that LARP, I'll kind of take it personally.

Thankfully, the costume worries keep my brain safely off the Luke worries. Worries like: I'm going out on an actual date-date with a totally nice guy. Worries like: I'm going to fumble around not knowing any of the people or the rules at this LARP and make a total fool out of myself.

Costume worries are way simpler.

Luke gets back to me two days later with a rough character concept. I'm playing a sorcerer from the Throne faction that goes by the name *Delilah.* The character comes with a caveat: a lot of it was improvised at the last second to fit in with existing plot. That means I'm going to have to let the gamemasters tell me what to do on occasion, in order to keep things running smoothly.

I'm used to having a full character sheet with plenty of stats—but instead, I've got a brief description of my faction and an email address for the head gamemaster, Corinna. I send an email off her way in a hurry, all but begging for solid costume tips.

The email I get back is... devilishly encouraging.

"Oh man," I tell Liv over dinner, while I read through it. "Luke is *so* gonna regret asking them to give me this character." I grin with barely-veiled glee.

Liv raises an eyebrow at that. I let her read the email, and she stifles a gasp. "Oh my gosh," she says. "You're not kidding."

I finish my soup and roll my shoulders. "All right. Costume-time starts now. I've got a *lot* of work to do."

6

EMILY

Those two weeks pass much more quickly than I expected them to do. Part of it is my ongoing discussions with Corinna via email; after the initial hurdle of having to pull another character out of thin air, she's gotten *very* excited about my costuming propositions. The more I elaborate on my plans, the more she sends back suggestions for character tweaks. Between us, I'm confident we're going to make Luke's game a living hell in the very best, most delicious way. I already owe this woman a beer and a high five, and I haven't even made it to her game yet.

Luke has started suspecting something is up, mostly because we've started texting every day, and I'm not trying *too* hard to hide my glee. As I get in the car Friday evening to head for the ranch, I close the door and pause to check my phone. The light is blinking yet again, and I grin.

LUKE: You're going to have to drop me a hint at some point tonight.

I snort and text him back.

EMILY: I don't have to do anything of the sort. You can stew in your curiosity a little bit longer.

His reply is almost instantaneous.

LUKE: Don't be so sure. I can interrogate you. I have my ways.

A delicious little shiver goes down my spine at that. *Mm.*

EMILY: By all means. Do your worst.

I set my phone aside and start up the car.

It's a good two-and-a-half hour drive out to the ranch, which is why almost everyone is heading up there on Friday night. The game technically starts on Saturday morning around noon, but I'm told there's going to be some casual roleplaying the night before, over dinner. There's a strict no-alcohol rule for the weekend, so I'm at least confident I won't be running into a repeat of my embarrassing evening at TowerCon.

In fact, I've planned ahead for the occasion—I went to work unusually dressed to kill. I'm wearing a loose backless shirt that shows off the one set of daring lingerie that I own. The forest-green lace is openly visible, and the shirt is easy to discard in a hurry. I work hard to keep this fine cosplay ass, so I've put it nicely on display with some black tights and high boots.

It's not an unreasonable outfit for the summer heat. But I'm sure it will convey my point to Luke quite nicely. That point being: I have *zero* intention of wasting this night with him on a couch.

It's well after sunset by the time I pull into the dusty parking lot just in front of the ranch. I make a mental note to wash the car before I give it back to Liv; I'm pretty sure it's currently a brownish-red dirt color. I can see the lights of the main building just a short distance ahead, up a sandy, winding walkway.

There's a message on my phone, of course. I pause to give it a look.

LUKE: I'm here. Give me a call when you arrive, and I'll help with your stuff.

I shake my head, bewildered. I still don't know what my libido is doing with itself. This man has been nothing but a perfect gentleman, and I'm *still* ready to tear his clothes off.

I mean, I'm not *complaining*. But it's definitely a new experience for me.

I dial Luke's number. He picks up by the second ring. "Hey," I mumble, feeling weirdly shy for a woman in a backless shirt. "I'm here."

"Excellent," Luke tells me. *"Your interrogation will begin shortly."* I choke back a laugh. I can hear the sound of people chatting excitedly in the background, but the voices fade as he heads outside.

"I should warn you," I say conversationally, "I once kept a secret from Finn for half a year. A few days is gonna be a piece of cake by comparison."

"Please," Luke sighs. *"Give me some credit. I am far more devious than Finn. And I'm going to have full access to you for almost three days."*

There's a knock on my car window, and I see him standing outside. There's a brief glow of his phone as he closes the line and slides it into his pocket. I stash my own phone and unlock the door, and he opens it for me. *Like a fucking gentleman.*

It's hard to see much of Luke in the darkness, but I

can tell he's generally well-dressed again, with another vest and tie. His hand is warm as he takes mine and helps me out of the car. I get a distinct whiff of that fantastic cologne, and my knees go a little bit wobbly.

This is going to be a *good* weekend.

"Hey there, Delilah," Luke says, with a hint of amusement in his voice.

I giggle like a teenager. "I'm gonna hear that *all* weekend," I tell him.

"It's true," he agrees. "But let me be the first to say it, before it becomes a cliche."

I can't help it. I reach out to grab him by the tie and drag him toward me. Luke lets out a surprised noise as I lean up to press my mouth to his. His hands come down to rest on my bare shoulders; his fingers brush the lace of my bra, and he groans into my mouth.

Two weeks of unresolved sexual tension flares up in a heartbeat. The next thing I know, I'm pressed back against my car, surrounded by that heady cologne. His teeth close lightly on my lower lip. I drag him closer, sliding my hands around to feel the muscles of his back. Our tongues slide against each other, and I let out a breathy moan.

My outfit has left an explicit invitation of exposed skin—but Luke's hands slide down to linger on my well-covered hips instead. I grab one of his hands and bring it up to my breast, and his breath chokes in his throat. He squeezes there obligingly, and I actually sigh in relief.

I didn't realize it until this moment, but I *desperately* needed this man's hands all over me.

The kiss gets a little rougher. His thumb brushes across my nipple through the material of my shirt, and I shiver in the summer heat. I *know* I can't take this too much further out in the middle of a parking lot, but it's suddenly incredibly hard to stop.

Thankfully, at least one of us has a modicum of self-control. Luke pulls back with a deep breath. "Holy fuck," he manages. "What was *that* for?" He pauses, bewildered. "Not that I'm *complaining*."

I suck on my aching lower lip for just a second, savoring the sting. "This is a date," I mumble with a grin. "You said so yourself."

Luke lets out a shaky laugh. "I didn't figure you for a dessert-before-dinner kind of woman," he says. "I like it."

"Oh," I breathe at him. "There's gonna be dessert." I run my fingers down his tie again. "God, I love these things. They're like ready-made leashes."

This time, I feel *him* shiver. "Well, uh. Good thing I brought a few," he says.

New headlights flash just behind us, and Luke eases away from me slowly before new company arrives. He clears his throat. "Uh... what can I carry?"

I lean back into the driver's seat to pop the trunk. I'm briefly disappointed that it's so dark out, because I *know* I'd otherwise be giving him a great view of my ass. "Careful what you wish for," I advise him. "I brought my whole makeup case."

"You forget," Luke says dryly. "I've *seen* your channel." He takes the heaviest stuff, and I'm left with just a single suitcase to carry. "Watch yourself at the curb," he advises. "It's a bit of a step up."

The main building is surprisingly nice for an old ranch. It's still rustic, but it's clearly been renovated, and it's fully air-conditioned. I can see a bunch of people in the mess hall sitting at a rough antique table, eating from a surprisingly fancy-looking buffet. For now, I head up a set of side stairs with Luke and walk to a room at the end of the hallway. He pulls out a key and lets us into a comfy-looking bedroom. There's a few pieces of artwork, a side desk, a couch... and a quilted king-sized bed that I intend to use to the fullest.

Luke sets my stuff down on the bed and turns, and I have to suck in my breath. It's true that he's wearing more of the same—a dark burgundy vest this time, and a set of slacks. But he's added a set of blood-red contact lenses. I'm not sure whether I'm more excited to nibble on him or give him eyeliner. Either way, he's an aphrodisiac for my inner cosplay-artist.

Those red eyes sweep up and down my body, and I'm pleased to see a similar reaction from him. Luke takes another deep breath. "I'm trying to remind myself I need to eat," he says.

"Hard same," I admit. "God damn. Are those contacts new?"

Luke blinks a few times at the reminder, and I can tell they are. "Yeah," he says. "It's my first time trying them out. I don't normally wear contacts, so I figured I'd see how I tolerate them for an hour or two tonight."

I turn to rummage in one of my suitcases and pull out a set of eye drops. "Two drops in each eye, whenever you get uncomfortable," I tell him. "If you start feeling like they're scratching at your eye, take them out pronto."

Luke shoots me a bemused look. "I somehow forgot I was here with a professional," he says.

He takes a second in the adjoining bathroom to put in a few eye drops. When he comes back out, he offers me an arm. "I'd offer to pay for dinner," he says. "But it's already included with the ticket."

I arch an eyebrow and slide my arm through his. "You paid for the ticket," I point out. Every inch of me tingles wherever we touch.

"Fair point," Luke acknowledges, as we head down the stairs. "But I *clearly* had ulterior motives."

I lean up toward his ear. "I am *counting* on your ulterior motives," I murmur there.

"Oof," Luke mumbles. "Have some pity. I really do want to introduce you to some people, but you keep appealing to the villain in me."

I chuckle at that. "I'll try to be nicer," I say. "Since I'm playing a good girl."

"Mm," Luke agrees. "Delilah. Throne faction. Veritable angel, both literally and figuratively. I hear we were childhood friends, before I went grimdark."

I can't help the wicked smile that crosses my lips at that. "We were," I say. "And I *so* want to believe there's still some good in you, Sebastian. I'm sure you're not as awful as all those other Sanguinist sorcerers."

"I *really* hope you haven't placed any money on that bet of yours," Luke tells me dryly.

One of the women at the mess table stands up and heads toward us, before I can answer. She's black-skinned, about my height, dressed in a sensible business suit and stylish flats. Her black hair is naturally frizzed, but she's dyed the very ends of it in a dark violet color. I frown at her—I'm almost positive I've seen her somewhere before, but I can't quite put my finger on it.

"Luke!" she says, with far too much brightness. "Look at you, already eviler-looking than last year!" She turns a suddenly devilish smile on me; our eyes meet, and I *know* I'm talking to Corinna. I can't help the secretive grin that crosses my face in reply. "And hello to you too, Emily." Corinna basically purrs out the sentence, vibrating with unabashed glee.

"Oh come *on*, Cor," Luke protests. "I know you've been plotting against me. You don't have to rub it in so hard."

Corinna presses a hand to her chest in mock offense. "Me? Plot? Against you?" She shakes her head. "It's almost as if that's my *job*. Like you paid me actual money for it and drove out to the middle of nowhere just so I could do it."

I disentangle myself from Luke's arm to offer out a hand. "It is *such* a pleasure to meet you in person," I tell Corinna. She shakes my hand, and I already feel like we've started an incredibly promising friendship. "I can't believe the amount of work you put into this thing. I only do my *own* costumes, and that's way more than enough to keep me busy."

Corinna grins. "The plot is way more work than the costumes," she tells me. "But I've got to say, I'm *thrilled* to have a professional cosplayer on this particular plot. If you don't take any pictures, I promise I will."

Something clicks into place in my brain then, and I gasp. "Oh, wow!" I manage. "That's where I've seen you before!" I shake my head. "You were the 1970's Wonder Woman at TowerCon last year, weren't you? The one with the bubble gum and the roller skates!"

Corinna's grin widens with genuine pleasure. "Aw," she says. "I'm flattered you remember. I just grabbed a bunch of stuff from some thrift stores and added some skates."

"You *did* win most creative costume," I point out. "Pretty hard to forget."

Luke blinks. "I didn't know you cosplayed, Cor," he says.

Corinna raises her eyebrows at him. "I'm a woman of mystery, Mr. Sebastian," she tells him. "Now go sit with your brother and eat. I've got evil plans to finalize with your girlfriend."

Luke and I both pause for a second at the word *girl-friend*. He glances toward me, as though to ask the unspoken question. I shrug. We let the moment pass. "Don't keep her for *too* long, Madam Storyteller," Luke tells Corinna. "I've got some other people to introduce her to."

Corinna smiles pleasantly. "Shoo," she tells Luke emphatically.

Luke gives me one last half-smile, before sliding his hands into his pockets and heading off for the other end of the table.

Corinna looks me in the eyes again, and my grin gets wider.

"Okay," she says. "I've got ten million things to do tonight. But I have the final background for Luke's character, and I wanted you to read a few things off it."

I barely resist the urge to rub my hands together like a super-villain. "This is the *best*," I tell her. "I just have to tell you that again."

Corinna blinks. "You really don't mind knowing the plot in advance?" she asks carefully. "I know it kind of spoils things for some players."

I shake my head emphatically. "Are you kidding?" I ask. "I'm going to tear his heart out and make him eat it. You told me he enjoys that sort of thing."

Corinna laughs. "I've been running for Luke for *four years*," she tells me. "He enjoys getting hurt almost as much as he enjoys being a bad man. It's gotten to where I have to up the ante every year." Corinna pulls a piece of paper from her pocket and hands it over to me. "This is what he knows about your character, verbatim. Read it over for me. Your plot is definitely going to break wide open about halfway through Sunday, but it might come out earlier if one of the other players gets super nosy. You've got until then to twist the knife as hard as you can."

I look down at the sheet she's given me. It's got a few short paragraphs on it.

What you know about Delilah, it says.

You and your brother Elisha grew up with Delilah. The three of you were basically inseparable—until the day you all came into your magic. Elisha and Delilah became Throne sorcerers, pledged to the side of the angels through a combination of fate and bloodlines. You were inducted into the Sanguinists. That was the end of any friendly bonds between you.

At first, you hoped to find a way to recover some relationship with Delilah—you were already madly in love with her when sheer bad luck drove that wedge between you. But as you learned more about your faction's dark path, you realized that your severed ties were for the best. Sweet little Delilah would be horrified to know the things you've done... and if you're completely honest with yourself, she's probably the only person left in this world who could convince you to abandon your faction's oaths. A meeting between you at this point could only irreparably damage you both.

Unfortunately, you've heard Delilah is back in town, along with your brother. On the one hand, it's probably best that you avoid them... but on the other hand, you've always been a glutton for punishment.

I smile down at the piece of paper. "Yeah," I say. "Oh yeah. I can work with this."

Corinna waggles her eyebrows at me. "I thought you might," she says. "Luke is convinced you're going to try to redeem him, by the way."

I flutter my eyelashes at her. "I'm sure I won't be dissuading him of the notion anytime soon," I tell her. "By the way—who's playing Elisha?"

Corinna turns and points toward the end of the table. Luke is sitting there chatting with a tall, broad-shouldered man in a loose plaid jacket. Objectively, I have to admit, he's something like a sexy lumberjack, with his blond hair and square jaw. But as nice-looking as he is, his good-natured smile and lack of formalwear do absolutely zilch for my *Labyrinth*-fueled complex.

Still, as I head over, I'm already feeling pretty good about the fact I'll be roleplaying a lot with Mr. Lumberjack. He's got a totally trustworthy-looking face, which I figure will make it way easier for him to help me surprise the hell out of Luke on Sunday.

"Well hello there," I say, as I slide into a chair next to Luke. "You'd be my fellow Throne sorcerer, wouldn't you?"

Luke tucks an arm around my waist, and I'm grateful for the contact. Much as I'm enjoying the people I've started meeting, I'm still feeling a little untethered around so many strangers. "This is Emily," Luke introduces me. "Emily, this is my brother Daniel."

I blink. "I thought his name was Elisha?"

Daniel smiles sheepishly at me. "You're not wrong," he says. "Elisha is my character's name. But I'm *actually* Luke's brother in real life." He pauses. "And in-game. Corinna decided to make it a thing."

I go from zero to beet red in a hurry. I'm suddenly extremely aware of Luke's arm around my waist. "Oh," I manage. "Oh, uh. Nice to meet you, Daniel."

Luke winces. "Sorry," he tells me. "I just realized I probably should have told you I'd have family around. Daniel and I don't really see a lot of each other, actually. He's been Canucking it up in the Great White North for most of my life."

Daniel smiles wryly at me. "We're technically half-brothers," he says. "I've probably seen about as much of Luke as you have. Though... I've played enough games with him at this point to know what I'm getting into this weekend."

Luke nods sagely. "I bond through villainy," he says. "Daniel here can't help but play the good guy. I think I've murdered him twice already."

"They were very impressive deaths," Daniel offers obligingly. "But there's not that many straight-up good guys in this game, so maybe this time won't be number three. My character is at least a *little* bit of an asshole, in spite of my normal preferences."

I relax very slightly at that. "Aw, Elisha," I say. "But you're such a perfect, self-righteous angel. I want to be more like *you*."

Luke rolls his red eyes exaggeratedly. Daniel grins,

and I remember that he *also* knows my character's biggest secret. "I'm sure you'll get the chance before the weekend is up," Daniel tells me cryptically.

Whatever little bit of tension we had between us quickly melts away as we eat dinner. Luke introduces me around to a bunch of people whose real names I quickly forget, but I make a few surreptitious notes about their characters on a notepad I brought with me.

I'm so absorbed in the friendly, energetic atmosphere that time passes more quickly than I expected. Soon, people start to trickle up to their rooms... and I'm a hundred percent ready to go to bed myself.

I mean. Not *by* myself. And I definitely don't intend to *sleep*.

I snatch Luke's hand and tug him gently away from a small group of players. "You're gonna want those contacts out," I tell him innocently.

Luke grins at the group. "That's my cue," he says to them. "I'll maim you all tomorrow, bright and early."

As we head upstairs, Luke slides his arm around my waist again. "You really want the contacts out?" he murmurs in my ear. His lips just barely tickle my earlobe.

I lick my lips. "Not... *right* away," I admit in a breathy voice.

The moment we close the door behind us, I shove Luke back onto the bed and crawl on top of him. My mouth comes down on his, and I know I'm about to have the hottest sex of my life.

"So... I'm *not* taking the couch?" Luke mumbles into my mouth. I can feel his smirk against my lips.

"I didn't wear this bra for nothing," I breathe. "Now... what are you gonna do about it?"

7

———

LUKE

*T*his is not at *all* the night I was expecting to have.

I've spent two long weeks reminding myself to be on my best behavior this weekend. I've got a hot, geeky woman sharing a room with me, and as much as I'm convinced she's into the idea of *eventually* getting back to that mind-blowing elf sex we started, I'm not ready to jeopardize the possibility just because I can't keep my hands to myself.

Two seconds into seeing her again, though, Emily is very soberly and consensually sliding her tongue into my mouth and pressing my hand to her *very* generous breast, and dinner has never felt so *fucking* long before.

You've been waiting to see a bunch of these people for a whole year, I remind myself forcibly, as I introduce Emily around. But she's already chatting up Corinna like they're old friends, and for some crazy reason neither of us has denied the idea that she's my girlfriend. To top it all off, Daniel already thinks she's great, and I can *tell* from the way he grins at me that he's thinking *good for you, Luke, what a nice girl!*

Emily, I have decided, is about as nice as I am. Which is to say: she's a hundred percent sweetness until she either puts on a costume or closes the bedroom door.

Speaking of which.

The woman in question is straddling me again, with her mouth hot against mine. Emily's wrapped my tie up in her hand—she's *definitely* got a thing for ties—and I'm pretty sure all the blood has left my head to travel south, because I'm feeling just a little lightheaded.

I run my hands up along her ass, savoring the feel of it in my palms. She's been wearing those tight black pants all night, and I've been *dying* to do this. Emily leans back into my hands with an approving moan, and I can see down that loose, backless shirt of hers. The bra she's wearing doesn't leave much to the imagination. I swear I can see her nipples dark against the lace. My cock jumps against her, and she smiles slowly, rubbing herself against me.

"Fuck," I groan. "I've been thinking about the way you felt in my lap about a hundred times a day."

Emily smiles languidly. "I've been trying to *remember* being in your lap," she admits. "I think it's starting to come back now."

I use my grip on her ass to flip her beneath me, and she lets out a pleased gasp. As forward as she's been, it hasn't escaped my notice that the lady likes being a little bit controlled.

And I *did* promise myself I'd be a gentleman.

I slide my hands up to her wrists, pinning them gently above her head. Emily writhes against me with an approving moan, and I smile slowly. "Are we going to need a safe word?" I murmur.

The hard shiver that goes through her body could mean a few different things—but the eager sound that comes out of her throat is unmistakable. "Yes *please*," Emily mumbles. "Oh god, I want you to hurt me just a *little* bit."

I tighten my grip on her wrists, and she arches instantly against me. I lean down to nibble at her ear. "Safe word first," I whisper with a grin.

Emily whimpers and lifts her legs around my waist. "Uh... fuck, I can't *think* for some reason," she moans. She licks her lips desperately. "Are you gonna laugh if I say *apples?*"

"No," I breathe into her ear. "I'm just going to fuck you so hard you see stars." I pause meaningfully. "Unless you say *apples*, of course."

Emily makes a high-pitched noise at that, and I can't help the low chuckle that escapes me. I'm quickly learning what turns this woman into putty, and it's *incredibly* satisfying to my male ego.

I hold her wrists with one hand and reach down to pull her shirt up above her bra. I was right—I can see her nipples against the dark green lace. They're pert and flushed and begging to be touched. I pinch one of them gently between my fingers, rolling it slowly. "I hear you're playing a good girl this weekend," I whisper in her ear. "Are you gonna be a good girl for me?"

"Jesus," Emily moans. "Oh, fuck. Yes I *am*." She lifts her hips against me again, imploring me to do more. "But only if you'll be mean to me, baby."

"Oh look," I murmur. "My specialty." I duck my head

and close my teeth on her neck—not hard enough to leave bruises, of course. I'd hate to ruin whatever costume she's got for tomorrow. I have to let go of her wrists to keep moving downward, but I've got her neatly pinned beneath me, so I figure that makes up for it. I close my lips around one of those lace-covered nipples, and she bucks into my mouth with a gasp.

Emily quickly tugs her shirt the rest of the way over her head, tossing it blindly aside. Her fingers dig into my hair as I lick and suck and lightly nibble at her breasts. I've been thinking about those breasts for two weeks now, after nearly getting my hands on them. They're just as round and firm and gorgeous as I remember.

I could spend a good long while admiring those breasts. But I'm a little hot and bothered, in spite of the air conditioning, and this tie is starting to feel tight. I trail my mouth back up toward hers and press her into the bed with a hard, punishing kiss. "I think we both need to be a little more naked," I mumble dazedly. "What do you think?"

Emily responds by pulling my tie free and fumbling with the buttons on my vest. Soon, she's got my shirt off, and the cold air hits my skin, cooling me down significantly. I help her pull off her boots—they're nearly as impractical as they are attractive—and before long, I've got her shimmying out of those tights. She's wearing a matching set of nearly-transparent panties, and I can already see a dark, wet triangle of hair between her legs.

No one's blackout drunk. The woman of my dreams is wearing see-through lingerie and not much else. It's an early night, and we've got a room to ourselves.

I check my annoying conscience. For once, it's giving me the all-clear.

My mouth comes down on hers again. I slide my hand down between us and rub my fingertips along the damp lace between her legs. Emily gasps and moans and lifts her hips again, while her hands fumble with the button on my pants. She slides the pants down my hips and tosses them aside just as I dip a finger beneath that lace, pressing it inside her.

"Yes yes *yes*," Emily whimpers against me. I push my finger deeper, and she tightens around it. Her fingers close on my cock, and I jerk into her hand with a sharp swear word.

She strokes me with a firm grip, holding my eyes with hers as she does. I slide another finger inside her. Her eyes darken attractively, and her lips part with a sharp intake of breath.

My pants are somewhere off to the side, but they're close enough that I'm able to grab a condom from their pocket.

I press the condom into Emily's hand, then reach up to close my fingers tightly in her hair. I jerk her head back, and she tightens sharply around my fingers again, moaning. I wait a second longer... but there's zero sign of any safe word. Emily pulls the condom open with trembling hands and slides it over my cock.

"*That's* a good girl," I breathe into her mouth. The words make her whimper again, and she guides me toward her entrance. I pull my fingers free and press my tip slowly inside her.

She's tight and hot and absolutely ready to be fucked. I pull sharply at her hair again and sink into her with a satisfied moan. Emily moans too, shifting to take me even deeper. I'm thinking about the way she begged me to hurt her *just a little*, so I close my teeth on her lower lip just hard enough to bruise.

It's a winning bet. Her hands slide up my back. Her fingernails dig into my skin. I shift my full weight on top of her, pinning her to the bed, and she shudders against me with satisfaction.

I take a few slow, leisurely strokes, enjoying the feel of her around me. Emily tests my weight, pressing up against me—but there's still no safe word, and I'm starting to think there isn't going to be.

"Rougher?" I murmur against her.

"You haven't even pulled out any hair yet," she rasps, with a sultry little smile. Emily drags her mouth across mine again, flicking out her tongue against me. "*Rougher.*"

I wrench her back by the hair and thrust harder, and she lets out a soft cry. "Like that," she whimpers. "Just like that, Luke. Oh my god."

I've got a good measure now, I think. I stop holding back quite so much. I'm normally a little tamer than this, but I don't mind adjusting. Besides which, she's soon openly begging and moaning my name, and every time she does it, I just get harder.

I let go of my self-control and *thoroughly* fuck the woman I've been dying to touch for two whole weeks.

Emily's voice rises higher and higher in pitch. Those nails dig into my back again. I'm probably going to have scratches; I really couldn't care less. I *do* cover her mouth with mine, since she's starting to get loud enough she might feel embarrassed tomorrow morning. Everyone here is a mature adult, but the walls aren't *that* well-insulated.

Her breath hitches, and her body trembles. I risk going a little harder, and she's nearly climbing me now, desperate for that last inch. I'm barely holding back myself. This woman *does* things to me, and I'm so fucking close to coming... but I want to feel her go first.

I'm pretty sure I know how to make that happen.

I tear my mouth from hers and press it to her ear. "Is that the cock you wanted, Julianna?" I murmur wickedly.

There's a shocked, strangled sound in Emily's throat. She arches against me, and her muscles clamp down on my cock. My vision goes white for a second, and then I'm coming too, moaning her real name this time. She's soft and trembling against me in all the right places, and I savor the feel of her underneath me, gasping and whimpering as she rides the orgasm I gave her.

"Oh fuck," Emily mumbles. "Ohhhh my god. Yes. That was." She takes another shaking breath, and I see her looking at me with glazed eyes. "Holy *hell.*"

My arms aren't supporting me anymore for some strange reason. I collapse onto the bed next to her, feeling more than a little dizzy. There's a hint of satisfying triumph in me too, as I drag Emily back into my arms.

Night one: incomplete sentences.

Tomorrow night, I'm aiming for *speechless.*

"You okay?" I mumble with a hazy grin.

Emily shivers in my arms for another minute or so, holding on tightly. Eventually, she nods with a breathless laugh.

It takes us a while to find the presence of mind to clean up. But Emily settles back next to me, gloriously naked, and I'm somehow looking forward to properly seducing her even more than before.

EMILY

I'm a pile of embarrassing goo. No, I can give myself a little more credit than that: I'm more like a Jell-O shot. I can hold myself together, as long as no one expects me to stand on my own. And I probably still taste fantastic.

Luke has fallen asleep next to me, but I'm still wrapped up in his arms. I'm feeling dangerously mushy and totally bewildered. I knew I was going to have the best sex of my life—but I somehow managed to wildly underestimate the meaning of the word *best*.

I know my preferences are just a *little* edgy for some guys. I was definitely expecting something... nicer? Sweeter? Okay, somehow it was rough *and* sweet at the same time, and my brain can't handle the apparent contradiction.

All I know is that I *definitely* need to do that again.

The very hot, very decent guy behind me tightens his arms on me, and I'm in huge trouble. My heart is doing a stupid dance in my chest like I've just won the lottery.

It's been two weeks! my rational brain screams at me. *This is literally the second time you've spent any real time with him in-person!*

I count everything up again carefully.

Hah, I think. *Third time. The coffee shop counts too.*

Shockingly, this does not do very much at all to reassure the little panicking voice in my head.

Weird David Bowie complexes aside, I don't do *stupid* in relationships. Yeah, I've sometimes made a few questionable choices on one-night stands, but I always listen to my instincts when I feel like a relationship's going bad. The combination of my traitorous libido and my smart long-term choices has put me in the very weird position of never dating anyone for very long.

Is this what a healthy relationship feels like? Does it just... immediately hit you in the chest and stubbornly lock into place like this? Am I supposed to feel like I need to desperately cling to this guy and refuse to let go?

Two. Weeks. My rational brain butts in again insistently.

Luke presses his lips sleepily to the back of my neck, and I tell my rational brain to shut the hell up.

I calm the butterflies in my stomach. I don't have to decide if I'm going to marry the man right this second, whatever Miserable Drunken Emily might think. I can take a breath. I've got two more days to figure out the next step here, which will probably just be *hey, let's keep dating and gaming and you can keep on with the mind blowing sex whenever the hell you feel like it.*

Yeah. That sounds like a good plan. That's a *rational* plan.

Somehow, I'm still feeling uncomfortably goo-like though, as I fall asleep next to him.

8

———

EMILY

*L*uke stumbles out of bed the next day around the same time I do, which is a nice change. I'm used to hearing Liv get up at ungodly o' clock, whistling cheerfully to herself like some goddamn cartoon princess.

I'm still admittedly a little goo-like when I hop into the shower with Luke. We're both such slowpokes that there's just no time for a tempting quickie. I have to settle for a few long, slow kisses and stupid grins.

Damn, he looks good just out of bed. He also looks good wet. I mean, who am I kidding—he's just delicious *all* the time.

"I just realized," Luke mumbles into my mouth, as the hot water slowly wakes us both up. "I never got any plot out of you last night."

I grin, running my hands up and down his wet body. "You didn't?" I murmur. "Mm. That's weird." I pause. "Better luck next time, I guess."

Luke pinches my ass, and I squeal with surprise.

"Next time," he promises, with a now-familiar, wicked grin.

Ugh. I think my insides are melting again.

I start pulling on my costume, such as it is. It doesn't take long for Luke to get dressed, and I catch him watching admiringly once or twice while he waits on me. "I'm getting a kind of girl-next-door, Catholic schoolgirl vibe from this costume," he observes.

I shoot him my most innocent smile and tighten my own striped tie. "I serve the divine Throne," I tell him piously. "What were you expecting, devil horns?"

Luke grins. "I don't know what I was expecting," he admits. "It sounded like you spent a decent amount of time on your costume. I mean... don't get me wrong, you're gorgeous. But I know what you can do with two whole weeks."

I raise my eyebrows slowly at him. "Someone doesn't know how to save the best for last," I say. "Day one is for exposition, sir. Today, I teach you what normal Delilah looks like. Tomorrow, you get to see a different side of her."

Today's makeup is understated; I'm mostly done up in natural colors, but I add some subtle white highlights to make myself look extra innocent and sweet. Luke's a good sport; he snaps a dizzying number of pictures of me for posterity, so I can do a few posts later. Afterward, I help him with his contacts and go to town on him with some eyeliner and lipliner. I can tell he's more than a little skeptical, but I am, as he's said, a *professional.*

I turn Luke around toward the mirror when I'm done, and he blinks. "What did you *do?*" he asks curiously.

I grin. "I sharpened the shape of your lips," I tell him.

"I gave you a subtle little sneer, so you've got resting villain face."

Luke laughs, and I can tell he's pleased with the outcome. "Okay," he admits. "I should have trusted you. You're making me into a believer."

"Damn straight," I tell him. I restack my makeup case and snap it closed. "If I can do rotten zombie flesh, I *think* I can do *evil blood sorcerer*."

Luke smirks at me. "*Evil* is such an out-of-character word," he says. "Sebastian would prefer the word *practical*. Maybe *principled*."

I arch an eyebrow. "*Principled?*" I repeat skeptically.

"Oh yes," Luke assures me. "Sanguinists just do the math. Sometimes, one innocent sacrifice can save a thousand other innocent lives."

It takes absolutely everything I have not to give anything away on my face. I force myself to look vaguely distressed instead. "I know you don't believe that, Seb," I tell him.

Luke presses a hand into the wall behind my head and leans down toward me. His red eyes glitter, and that eyeliner is making me predictably hot and bothered. "What you know could fill a thimble, you little airhead," he tells me cruelly.

I know I've got a screw loose in my head. But god, that was *hot*.

"So that's how it's gonna be?" I ask him with a slow smile.

Luke arches an eyebrow. "Too much?" he asks, in his more usual, laid-back tone. "I can scale it back some."

I have to work not to lick my lips. The last top coat over my soft pink lip stain is still setting. "Oh no," I manage. "That's *perfect*. I'm gonna have to work on my fake tears." I pause. "*After* the mascara is dry."

We're not in-character *yet*, all joking aside. Luke offers out his arm, and I take it with a grin.

I might have some weird issues—but at least I'm dating a guy with *complementary* weird issues to mine.

Two weeks, my brain insists.

I roll my eyes and consciously turn off Emily for the day. It's time to eat breakfast and turn into Delilah for a bit.

Shit. I sigh to myself. *Now I have that song stuck in my head too.*

LUKE

Everyone's reading and re-reading their character backgrounds over breakfast, and I'm no exception. I must have read the section on Delilah a hundred times by now, but I still can't figure out if there's a clue to Emily's plot in there that I've somehow missed.

Not that I *really* want to figure it out ahead of time. Corinna knows how to write a compelling plot, and she seemed particularly excited about this new character, once she got over her initial wail of *why would you do this to me two weeks before game, you son of a bitch.*

Corinna once gave me a black eye and then threw up all over me. I think it's fair to call us even now.

Still, it's a *little* disappointing when Corinna calls the start of game and I have to wiggle Emily out from under my arm. I'm already getting addicted to all these little casual touches between us. I'm going to feel a little Emily-starved while I'm playing Sebastian today, which is... I guess, kind of appropriate. I decide to sneak in the occasional touch anyway, once we've had our first run-in. I'm getting a very *want what I can't have* vibe off this character, and now that I'm in costume, I can feel Sebastian starting to come to life properly.

I catch my reflection once or twice on the way to my starting room. I'm not sure whether I look mildly goth or maybe eighties glam-rock. Either way, Emily looked like she wanted to devour me this morning, so guyliner it is.

What *did* she mean about the movie *Labyrinth,* anyway?

I set the thought aside for a later date. I'm the only Sanguinist in the game, but I'm starting off with a few loose allies in the room. Out-of-character, I've played with all of them before, and we get along just fine. In-character, they're all at least a little bit uncomfortable with me. Silhouette, our Ghostspeaker, keeps glancing warily over at me. Restless, the Hollow, keeps himself subtly between me and the rest of the group, as though I might be unexpectedly dangerous.

"Something is very wrong in this city," Silhouette whispers. She's a tall, pale woman dressed mostly in white. We all have to lean in just a little bit to hear her. "I can't get the spirits to talk to me. I can't even find most of them."

"Most of them?" Restless asks. "What about the ghosts you *did* find?" He's a bronze-skinned man, about the same height as Silhouette, done up with dozens of swirling temporary tattoos. I played opposite him last year, actually—he brutally murdered me. With my enthusiastic consent, of course.

Silhouette looks down. "I managed to find one spirit,"

she murmurs. "Something... tore her apart. I couldn't get anything coherent out of her. She just kept taking about a black gate."

I frown at that. Clear plot hook, if ever I heard one. "Where did you find her?" I ask calmly.

Silhouette's eyes flicker toward me. "Reunion Tower," she says softly. "She was hiding all the way at the top. I got a bad sense from the place, but it's not quite within my wheelhouse."

I shrug. "Maybe one of the rest of us will have better luck," I observe.

Restless shoots me a thin smile. "Not you," he says. "Not unless we've got no other choice."

I smile back. "I don't *always* have to kill people to cast spells, you know," I tell him.

Restless shakes his head. "Not the issue," he tells me. "The Throne has people in town right now. If they catch a whiff of blood magic, it's gonna be a headache and a half. You know those self-righteous pricks."

I narrow my eyes. "Which *specific* self-righteous pricks are we talking about?" I ask.

Silhouette starts absently humming *Hey There, Delilah*. I do my best to look abruptly uncomfortable.

Restless grins. "Yeah. Her and Elisha. You think they'll start up a good, old-fashioned inquisition while they're in town?"

I cross my arms and look away. "Delilah doesn't do inquisitions," I mutter. "I'm pretty sure she just asks pretty please with a cherry on top or something." I shake my head. "Elisha, on the other hand... he can come try to pull a Cain and Abel anytime he damn well pleases. I'm not going to start trying to make him happy *now*."

Restless shrugs. "Have it your way, bloody bones," he tells me. "Just don't expect me to stand between you and an angry angel."

I shoot him a narrow smile. "I don't expect you to stand between me and a stiff breeze," I reply. "But I know who you'll come running to if you want someone to disappear."

His eyes flash at me. It's a not-so-subtle jab. Sebastian assassinated someone for Restless a few years ago, and it's been blackmail material ever since.

I mean... *allies* is a really loose term in this game. That's part of what makes it so fun.

Silhouette sighs. "Let's keep it marginally pleasant for a few hours, at least," she says. "We have work to do, and we'll do it better together."

"I'm always pleasant," I lie evenly.

Restless scoffs at that.

Silhouette's player sneaks out to find a gamemaster so we can go properly ghost-hunting, and I start considering ways to lure my date into a scene with me as soon as possible.

* * *

Three scenes in, Corinna has run us through a few creepy investigative clues that ultimately lead—of course—to an old ranch outside of town. It makes the whole thing feel a little more in-the-moment for a bit.

Corinna settles herself into a rocking chair outside and pretends to be an old woman on the premises. She's got a dozen or so people to play today, so she's not wearing any particular costume. Instead, she just smiles at us eerily as we approach.

"By the way," Corinna adds, as we get closer. "I'm covered in blood from head to toe. It doesn't seem to bother me at all."

There are five people in our current group in total, including me. Four sets of eyes turn toward me at once. "This is *all* yours," Restless says.

"I get it," I say, with mock sympathy. "Old ladies can be terrifying. I'll make sure she doesn't have a scary handbag to hit you with."

Restless presses his lips together, trying to look angry. I can tell his player's just trying not to laugh, though.

I stride closer toward Corinna. The others huddle in closer out-of-character to listen in, even though their characters have stayed back a healthy distance. I put on a brief show for them. "Oh look," I mutter in a stage voice. "There's someone covered in blood. Better send the Sanguinist. I fell and scratched my knee and now I'm bleeding—better grab the Sanguinist. Is that tomato juice or blood? We clearly need a Sanguinist, god forbid someone just taste it—"

"You are late, Sanguinist," Corinna rasps at me in a low, croaking tone.

I stop dead in my tracks.

"...okay," I acknowledge. "Maybe this one needs a Sanguinist. What do I know." I eye her suspiciously and raise my voice to address her. "I don't guess that's tomato juice."

Corinna does a fair imitation of a cackling old lady. "One or a thousand, Sanguinist," she says. "We don't care which it is."

I consider her warily. It's clearly a reference to the Sanguinist philosophy. *Sacrifice one to save a thousand.* "I think I'll go find a lawyer before I answer," I joke.

"We have a few with us," Corinna cackles again. "But they are otherwise occupied."

I cross my fingers visibly. It's the official game signal that I'm speaking out-of-character. "I want to check the way this old lady's body is functioning," I tell Corinna. "Is her heart beating? Blood flowing normally? That sort of thing."

Corinna smiles. "Her heart is *not* beating," she says. "You're pretty sure the blood she's wearing is her own. Something made her bleed it out through her pores."

One of the players listening in makes a disgusted noise. I take in the news with exaggerated equanimity. "Huh," I mutter. "Look at that." I turn around. "Hey Sil!" I call out. "This one's dead. That makes her *your* problem."

Silhouette slinks forward reluctantly. I wind a friendly arm around her shoulders, incidentally shoving her forward. "Creepy dead old lady," I summarize for her. "Knows I'm a Sanguinist on sight. I'm thinking... evil spirit? That, or a *really* bad case of food poisoning."

Silhouette's player gives the out-of-character sign. "Is she a spirit?" she whispers.

Corinna knits her brow. "I can't hear you," she tells Silhouette apologetically. "You're gonna have to speak up out-of-character, sweetheart."

Silhouette giggles at herself and clears her throat. "Is she a spirit?" the player asks again—more loudly this time, and less breathy.

Corinna nods. "She's... definitely something *like* that," the gamemaster replies. "She's not a ghost... but she's something without a native corporeal form. Probably not even a *she*, so much as an *it*. Your usual magic might work halfway against this thing, but it's not quite on your wavelength." Corinna pauses. "And, on that note! I need you guys to freeze time for a second. I've got to go retrieve some people."

We settle down into the other chairs around us for a second. Silhouette's player gives me a curious look. "What do you think?" she asks. "Black gate, wrecked ghosts, evil spirit...*ish* thing. Any theories yet?"

I *hm*. "It's still early Saturday," I say. "But I'm getting a very demonic vibe here. That, or maybe something Lovecraftian."

Restless heads inside and comes back out with a few bottled waters to pass around. "My money's on demons," he says. "We did a whole *Call of Cthulhu* plot two years ago. Corinna doesn't like to repeat herself that quickly."

"Ah," I say sagely. "Excellent deduction work, my dear Sherlock."

Restless grins at me. "Are we gonna throw down before the end of game, you think?"

I chew on that. "Maybe," I acknowledge. "Right now, though, I'd say Sebastian thinks he's got you under control. You'd have to do something a little dangerous to make him decide you're easier to kill than blackmail."

Silhouette's player raises her eyebrows with glee. "Blackmail?" she says. "Ooh. Bad boy, Restless. What did you *do*?"

I wave a hand at her. "That was a slip on my part. Pretend you didn't hear that, you nosy ghost spy."

Silhouette holds up her hands. "Already forgotten,"

she assures me. "Unless, of course, a little ghost happens to hear something about it in-game. *Then,* we have fun."

Restless spreads his hands. "I will do my utmost to make sure I say something stupid in front of a ghost," he assures Silhouette. "No promises, since human spirits seem to be light on the ground at the moment."

Corinna returns at this point, leading another group of players toward us. Emily and Daniel are with her, and I instantly start paying closer attention. Emily catches my eyes and blushes just a little bit. It's even more adorable than it might be otherwise, given that she's wearing that soft makeup and that girl-next-door look. I shoot her back my most villainous smirk.

"...this is where your spell would have led you," Corinna is telling the new group of players. "Majorly bad spiritual mojo, right around here." She looks back toward us and mimes surprise at me. "Oh look, Sebastian! Wait... no. He's bad mojo, but he's not *the* bad mojo you were looking for. That would be the bloody old lady in the rocking chair he's currently talking to."

Corinna heads back toward the rocking chair and settles herself back into her creepy old lady vibe. "When I call time in, the other group will just be coming around the side of the building," she tells us. "All right—time in!"

"What in god's name is going on?" Daniel demands. He strides over and grabs me by the arm. "I should have known *you* were involved with this."

I sigh exaggeratedly—but my eyes are still on Emily, behind him. "You've caught me, Elisha," I say. "I spilled tomato juice all over this poor woman."

Silhouette's player coughs lightly to cover a snicker.

Corinna turns her eyes toward Elisha. "Favored Son,"

she hisses. "Are you here to pay your debts? We are waiting."

Daniel makes the out-of-character sign. "Demon?" he asks Corinna, as though he already knows the answer. I get the impression their group has been following a very different investigative trail than ours.

Corinna smiles at him. "Demon," she confirms.

Daniel pulls a notecard from his pocket and holds it up as though it's something to be feared. "Don't talk to me, serpent," he commands.

Corinna pulls back from the notecard with narrowed eyes. The words *Throne Talisman* are written on it. She slinks back further and turns her eyes toward Emily. "Little lamb," she gurgles, now exaggerating her disgusting tone. "Come and kiss us, little lamb—"

Emily's eyes widen in abject horror.

I reach out quickly and touch Corinna's shoulder. "Anyone mind if I end this encounter abruptly?" I ask cheerfully.

Corinna grins at me. "I've done what I needed," she says. "Up to everyone else."

There's a general chorus of agreement. Corinna nods and turns back to me. "How are you ending this, Sanguinist?" she asks me.

"I pull a pocket knife and draw my own blood, along my arm," I say. "As I spatter it against the old woman, her body melts grotesquely and dissolves into an ugly red mist. The demon has no body left to possess, at least for the moment."

"Gross," Silhouette's player says admiringly. "I dig it."

I take a shallow bow. "Apparently, I'm into body horror this year. I'll be here all night." I straighten up again. "On time in, I'll still obviously be staring at Delilah, if anyone would like to notice."

"Staring how?" Reckless asks me.

I consider that. "How socially perceptive are you?" I ask.

Reckless smiles slowly. "I've got a tattoo that gives me heightened senses," he says. "What do you *want* to give me?"

I take a small step toward him and lower my voice. "That thing threatened Delilah," I murmur. "I went from zero to murder in two seconds flat."

Reckless raises his eyebrows. "That is *fantastic* information," he says softly. "How do you feel about reverse blackmail?"

"I'm for it, in general." I grin. "Think it over and pitch me a plot development later." I step back to where I was standing before. "All right. Time in."

Corinna amps up the gross gurgling noises. Players instantly recoil from the rocking chair, reacting with varying levels of horror and disgust. As promised, I keep my eyes on Emily, who's pressed her hand over her mouth. Reckless, in turn, watches me.

"What are you doing, you *idiot!*" Daniel demands. He pulls me back by the arm. "We were going to trap it and banish it back to hell! Now it's untethered! It could haunt this place for the next hundred years!"

I jerk my arm out of his grip. "First, you call me a demon-summoner, and now you want me to wait for your orders," I observe coldly. "I'm getting mixed signals, Elisha. I'm not in the mood for *he loves me, he loves me not.*"

Daniel really tries to keep a straight face. But there's a

reason he doesn't play provocative characters very well. He is really, truly, *far* too nice. He's never been a telemarketer; he can't even pretend to be evil. Instead, he has to pause to snort into his hand.

I look over Daniel's shoulder at Emily. "Look who else is here," I say in a dark tone. I crook my finger at her. "Hey there, Delilah." I drop my voice to a sharp, bitter hiss. "Why don't you come and kiss us, little lamb?"

Emily covers her face and starts giggling in horror. "Oh my *god*," she says out-of-character. "You are so fucking awful."

I grin. "You love it," I say. "Come on, I want to see a reaction."

"Okay," Emily gasps. "I'm about to do my best *oh my god, is Seb actually going to murder me* face. I don't know how well I can actually act it out, because you just fucking blue-screened me for the day."

I decide to take that as a point of pride.

We slide back into character. Emily has arranged her face into an approximation of fear. Daniel's got himself more-or-less under control, so he grabs my arm again and spins me around. "Are you deranged?" he demands.

"Always," I reply, straight-faced. "But really, I'm just *thrilled* to see you both again. I'd say we should do coffee, but I don't trust you not to bless mine and watch me choke."

I love Daniel. I really, actually do. But the poor man cannot banter worth a damn. He shakes his head wordlessly instead, searching for a halfway-decent comeback. I take pity and toss him a more straightforward line instead. "What are you doing here, anyway?" I ask him.

"You already knew you were hunting demons, apparently, which is more than *we'd* figured out so far."

Daniel narrows his eyes at me—but he relaxes slightly and takes a step back. "I don't particularly want to work with you," he says. "But for something this serious... maybe it's necessary. We should at least go somewhere safer and share some information."

"Agreed," Silhouette whispers from behind me. "As long as the Throne can avoid smiting anyone for an hour or two."

Daniel bristles. "We're not irrational," he snaps. "As long as no one does *blood magic* in front of us again, we should be fine."

"More information-sharing, please," I drawl. "Less moralizing." I fix my eyes on Emily again and take a step past Daniel.

Emily flinches as I come closer. I smile coldly and reach out to brush her cheek.

"I've got blood on my hand," I whisper, with a wicked smile.

Emily swallows hard. She straightens slowly though, and sets her jaw. "I'm pretty sure that's not hygienic," she informs me. She's left a little tremble in her voice though. "You're... still bleeding, Seb. Do you need stitches?"

I consider her for a moment. *This is a redemption plot line,* I decide. Corinna turned my date into a sweet, wholesome little love interest to try and tempt me back to the light side.

I might play along this time. But I *definitely* intend to make everyone involved work their asses off for it.

"That depends," I say, with a devilish smile. "Are you too scared to kiss it better now, Dee?"

Emily swallows again. But she reaches up to curl her fingers around my hand. Slowly and deliberately—without once ducking my stare—she brings the inside of my wrist up to her lips and kisses it.

My pulse jumps like a jackhammer. I can tell she knows it too, based on the little smirk that crosses her lips. I can't tell whether that's an Emily smirk or a Delilah smirk. Probably doesn't matter.

"That's not where I'm hurt, Dee," I whisper.

Emily blinks slowly at me. "I can't kiss you where you're *really* hurt, Seb," she tells me. She drops my hand, and I feel a surge of instinctive disappointment. I could go for a hundred more little touches from her like that. "If you want stitches," she says softly, "you'll have to ask me nicely." Her eyes go cold. "Otherwise... you can keep fucking bleeding."

The words hit me like a cold splash of water. I feel my jaw drop.

Emily smiles prettily at me, and turns to walk away.

9

____

EMILY

 have only a split second to savor the *priceless* look on Luke's face before I turn to walk away. But I've got a perfect picture of it in my head, preserved for posterity.

Our two groups merge and start comparing notes. Over the course of the rest of the day, we discover that the *black gate* is actually a portal to hell. Naturally, it's about to crack wide open. We're not yet sure how to stop that, but by the time dinner rolls around, we've dug up the remnants of some ritual that got used the last time this danger threatened. Tomorrow will probably consist of us knitting all our clues together and actually conducting the ritual.

As our groups interact, I can tell Luke's got absolutely zero clue what to do with me now. He prevaricates between casting confused looks at me from across the room and hovering just out of arm's reach.

One of the players in Luke's group—a sorcerer named Reckless—looks like he's ready to break out a bag of popcorn and settle in to watch. Just before dinner, as Luke is distracted by his brother, Reckless heads over my way and draws me aside into another room.

"I get the feeling we should talk, *Dee*," Reckless murmurs.

I wrench myself away from him and narrow my eyes. "Don't call me that unless you're looking for a fight," I tell him. "Is that what you're here for?"

Reckless raises his hands, as though to fend me off. "Not at all," he says. "I've got no bones with the Throne. But I saw you knock the air out of a fucking blood mage with a few words and a smile. I've got to admit, I'm feeling *far* more impressed with you than your reputation would suggest."

I smile again coldly. "Does this conversation have a point?"

Reckless raises an eyebrow. "That depends," he says. "There are things I want that you might be able to give me. I'm willing to play ball for those things. The question is: is there something *you* might need from a Hollow, little Throne?"

I chew visibly on my lower lip. I have to decide how much I want to give away about my plot on day one. "What I want is way bigger than you can handle," I tell him finally.

Reckless spreads his hands. "Why don't you try me and find out?" he asks.

I shake my head. "I don't know where you got the idea I was this much of a moron," I tell him. "But you should second-guess your sources. I don't know you from Adam. Hell... I trust *Seb* more than I trust you, right now. And believe me, that's saying something."

Reckless smiles slowly. "Just tell me one thing," he says. "Are you enemies with Sebastian?"

I answer without a second's hesitation. "We're enemies," I say. "He's just too stupid to realize it."

His smile grows at that. "Maybe you think a Sanguinist is too much for me," he says. "But between the two of us at once—"

I cut him off. "If you so much as scratch Sebastian, I'll tear your soul from your body and feed it to one of those demons."

Reckless blinks. "You just said—"

"I *know* what I just said." I smile pleasantly. "Both of those things can be true at the same time." I shake my head. "Tomorrow's ritual requires a Sanguinist. If you let your personal business get in the way of the Throne's success, I won't be the only one looking to feed you your own essence. After the ritual, you can do whatever you want."

Reckless considers me for a long moment. I'm feeling a little nervous, so I bring up the out-of-character sign. "Too harsh?" I ask sheepishly.

Reckless smiles and switches out-of-character. "No, no," he assures me. "You're totally fine. I'm just fishing for information anyway—I didn't really expect an alliance."

I purse my lips and remember his comment to Luke about heightened senses. "Uh... I can drop some information if you want?" I offer. I'm not used to the total lack of rules here, but I've gotten the impression that this particular group of players leans toward being generous with each other.

"Whatever you're good with," Reckless says. I can tell he's being careful. I'm the new player, and he doesn't want to steamroll me. But even if this is my first live-action game, it's far from my first roleplaying game.

I chew on my lip and try to think up some interesting morsel of information that won't totally spoil Corinna's plot. "…I smell more than a little bit like blood," I say finally. "But I'm not visibly bleeding. I'm wearing some makeup, and I'm probably not very healthy-looking underneath it."

Reckless rubs at his chin. "If I check you specifically for blood magic," he says, "will I find some?"

"I'm not sure on that," I admit. "You'll want to check with Corinna. But I'd guess it's a yes. I'm carrying an item that's associated with blood magic."

"The Throne is messing around with blood magic?" Reckless drawls. "I'm just *shocked* and *appalled*." His eyes glitter. "All right. Any issues if I spread this around to a few people? Not to Sebastian, of course—though he might find out anyway."

I shake my head. "Go for it," I tell him. "Everything's going to be really obvious like halfway through the day tomorrow."

Reckless reaches out to shake my hand in an exaggerated, business-like manner. "It was a pleasure sneaking information from you," he informs me. "I look forward to speculating wildly on the implications and eventually being proven totally wrong."

We return just in time for dinner, when Corinna calls the official end of day one. We're still allowed to do scenes if we want, but nothing super plot-worthy that might involve her input. A few of the players who still feel like roleplaying coalesce at the far end of the table, but Luke is at the other end, loosening his tie. I slide into a chair next to him and wriggle underneath his arm with a sigh. It's more of a relief than I expected, being able to touch him again. We're still too standoffish in-character for me to do things like this.

Luke tightens his arm on me and smiles, and that's *also* weird. His character isn't capable of nice smiles like that, and I'm having a moment of dissonance now. "Long day already," he observes. "Sorry we didn't end up hanging out too much."

"Mm, well," I murmur. "We've got all evening."

"That's true," Luke muses. "And technically, I can interrogate you about plot *in-character* now." He arches an eyebrow, and I'm at least halfway sure that's a come-on.

I give him a slow, sexy smile. "What a coincidence," I tell him innocently. "Delilah was going to go find Seb tonight. To... talk."

Luke coughs on a laugh. "Why do I feel like I'm about to get murdered by the sweetest little sorcerer in the game?" he mumbles.

I bat my eyelashes and reach up to stroke his jaw. "I guess you'll just have to find out," I tell him. My fingers brush along his stubble, and he shivers.

"I'm always up for a risk," Luke says hoarsely. He grabs my hand and presses his lips lightly to my palm. That little kiss zings through me with astonishing strength, stealing my breath in a way that's never happened before. I can feel my whole body thrumming with dizzy anticipation.

I have never been this turned on before in my life. It's a fantastic feeling, but it's also... confusing. I've got *feelings* mixed up in that excitement that don't belong in a two-week relationship. I feel a little bit like I'm in a car driving full tilt toward a cliff.

I find myself searching Luke's face for any hint that he's feeling similar—but he's always so pleasant that I find him difficult to read.

And if he *was* going through the same crazy thoughts? Would that make it better or worse?

I genuinely don't know.

Luke leans down to kiss me—just the lightest, most innocent, most comfortable kiss—and I can't bring myself to care anymore. I can deal with the crazy tomorrow.

Tonight, I need this man naked again.

* * *

We end up calling it an early night, to no one's surprise.

As we head into our room, I'm deeply tempted to shove Luke down on the bed again and get this insanity out of my system immediately. But I had a *plan* when I was thinking up how to approach his character tonight, and the only thing that sounds even more delicious than sex right now is roleplaying *and* sex. Two of my favorite things.

Luke leans down to brush his lips over mine again as soon as the door is closed. He's warm, and he smells *amazing*, and my willpower is waning. Thankfully, one of us has his head on his shoulders. "You said Delilah was coming to see *Sebastian*, and not vice-versa," he murmurs. "This, I want to see."

I suck in a shivering breath. I'm so desperate to get my naked body against his, it feels like an addiction. The worst part is, I'm not sure whether that feeling is me, or my character, or both. Still—I somehow manage to step back and smooth down my shirt. I clear my throat and look down. "I guess we're all actually staying at the ranch, in-character," I mumble. "So... it wouldn't be too hard to find his room."

Luke crosses his arms and leans himself against the wall. I suspect he's doing it to prevent himself from touching me. He's still got those red contacts in, and that hint of a sneer I gave him earlier. He slips right back into character as though he was never himself at all. "Don't tell me you got lost on your way to my brother's room," he drawls. "Or are you here to lecture me?"

That invisible wall is back up between us—the one that kept us from touching each other all day. But I'm more than ready to knock it down.

"Would you *stop* being an asshole for just a few minutes?" I hiss at him. "With everything that's going on, you really want to do this?" I snap my hand out to grab him by the tie, because it's *there,* and I need to touch him. He blinks as I drag him down to eye level, genuinely startled. "Think really hard, Seb. If this was the last thing you ever said to me, would you be okay with that?"

Luke stiffens at that. The next thing I know, he's got me shoved up against the wall. I can feel the heat of his body, just inches from mine. "What the hell is that supposed to mean?" he grits out.

I've still got my hand curled in his tie. It's trapped between us, pressed against his chest. My breath's coming short. I feel a little dazed, and it must be showing on my face, because Luke eases back with a blink. "Uh..." He looks suddenly sheepish. "Should one of us be saying *apples*? I didn't hurt you, did I?"

I shake my head breathlessly. Somehow, I manage to swallow again. "*Please* keep going." I'm not too proud to beg at this point. Him and that eyeliner and the way he's got me backed up against this wall are hitting every one of those loose screws in my head. I need more of this, or I swear, I'm going to explode.

Luke leans his face down closer to me with a sly smile. "Well... technically, I just asked *you* a question," he murmurs. "So where were we?"

I close my eyes and suck in my breath. It's hard to think with him *right there*, hitting all my buttons at once, but I can do this. *What was the question again?* Oh. *He asked what I meant by... last thing he'd ever say... so on and so forth.*

"I meant..." My voice trembles a little on the words. "We're doing dangerous things tomorrow. There's no guarantee we'll all walk away from it in one piece."

Luke brushes my cheek with his fingers. I open my eyes, and see him staring down at me like he has no clue what to do with me. Slowly, he puts his thoughts together again. "I'm not a toy, Dee," Luke whispers to me. "I'm very dangerous to play with."

His fingers trail down my neck—down my front— now caressing their way along my thigh. "If you want someone to tell you it's going to be all right," he murmurs, "go talk to Elisha." He twists his hand in the fabric of my skirt, sliding it up to a deliciously indecent height. "If you want someone to make you *scream*... well. I guess I can oblige. For old times' sake."

Luke's hand travels up my bare thigh, and I swear I'm

going to cry if he doesn't keep going. I let out a soft whimper, and he smiles. "I wonder if that's fear," he muses. "Or... is the good little girl really just a little bit... *naughty.*" His finger brushes the damp fabric just over my slit, and I gasp. From the hot look in his eyes, I can tell he's noticed how soaking wet I am already.

"If that's all you want," I rasp out, "go ahead and take it."

Luke angles his head to press his lips against my ear. "If you want something," he whispers. "Ask me for it." He sucks lightly on the shell of my ear, and a little moan escapes my throat. He smirks against my skin.

"I want..." I'm breathless and dizzy and now feeling oddly sentimental. There *is* something I want. Something my character wants. For the moment, it's the same thing. "I want you to admit you care," I whisper.

Luke's finger is just sliding its way beneath the fabric of my panties. But he stops at that. I hear his breath hitch. "You want me to lie to you?" he murmurs finally.

I reach up to dig my fingers into his hair, dragging his face back to mine. "Yeah," I breathe. "Lie to me."

I'm not sure who moves first. Either way, his mouth is on mine—hot, demanding, *desperate.* The wall between us is gone, and it feels *incredible.* Luke's other hand finds my hair, wrenching me harder into the kiss. His body pins me to the wall. That finger slides inside my panties, instantly pressing deep inside of me. I cry out into his mouth, and he bites down on my lower lip.

I have to hold onto his tie for dear life. Every inch of me is flushed and tingling. His fingers leave my hair to start prying open my shirt, and if one of those buttons snaps away entirely, I really can't bring myself to give a damn. His hand slides inside the shirt to squeeze my breast, and I arch into his palm with a gasp. I start fumbling with his clothes, searching for bare skin to touch.

Luke's vest hits the floor. I pull open his shirt and run my palms along his chest, and he lets out a hiss of white-hot pleasure. His finger curls inside me, and I moan with a mixture of excitement and impatience. I thought he might make me beg a little bit more—but he's nearly as far gone as I am. He leans into my touch like a drowning man who's just come up for air.

Luke pulls his finger free just long enough to peel my panties off me entirely. He presses a condom into my hand again, and I rush to unbutton his pants, shoving them back so I can take his cock into my hand. He's so rock hard, it's easy to roll the condom onto him, even with my hands trembling.

He grabs my face in his hands and forces me to look him in the eyes. Red eyes. Smudged black eyeliner. I'm literally going to combust in this man's pretty, villainous hands.

"*Now*," Luke growls against me. "You're going to scream for me."

He slams his cock inside me with one hard stroke, and oh *yes*, I scream into his mouth. That impossible hunger I've been feeling gets filled all at once, and I *still* need more.

He holds my eyes while he fucks me, and it's so intense I'm hitting new levels of emotion. It's like scratching an impossible itch I didn't even know I had. I reach up to caress his jaw, and he hisses in his breath like I've burned him—but he leans into it again, instead of pulling away. It occurs to me that we're still fighting each other. His character is trying to pretend this is meaningless. But I'm slowly destroying his defenses with every little touch.

Luke is playing a villain for me, but he's intentionally playing to lose. And I'm eating it up with a spoon.

I soften my touch and run my fingers up through his hair again. He shudders visibly. That punishing kiss relents a bit, and I sigh into him. The kiss is still hard and hungry, but there's a note of sincerity to it that wasn't there before. I lift my thigh up along his waist, taking him in deeper with the next stroke. He moans into me, and the sound is nearly better than the feel of his cock inside me. I *earned* that sound, damn it.

He still fucks me hard—but it's slower, more drawn-out, more *satisfying*. Luke slides his hand through my hair, but this time it's just to feel it in his fingers. "*Fuck,*" he breathes. "This is... a bad idea..."

I lift my hips to meet him on the next thrust, and we both moan. Every time he slides inside me, the tingling on my skin gets stronger. I'm already so close to coming, and I know it's going to be so *good*.

I look him in the eyes again. He's hazy-looking, and I'm pretty sure we're both about to lose our minds.

"Lie to me, Seb," I whisper to him.

Luke licks his lips. He kisses me again, and I almost don't hear his murmur.

"*God*, I love you," he mumbles.

It's the absolute *last* thing I'm expecting to hear. The tingling on my skin surges, and I orgasm with a heady shock. I feel him come inside me too. I'm absolutely untethered for a second, floating in a haze of incredible satisfaction and warm confusion.

I barely manage to tumble into bed. My legs are shaking. Somehow, I end up naked in Luke's arms and he's kissing me again, like he needs me in order to breathe.

I'm kissing him back the same way. There's a deep, overwhelming warmth bubbling up inside me. The rational voice in my head doesn't even try to protest this time.

No one's ever said those words to me in quite that way before. I'm already replaying them in my head, holding onto them like they're impossibly precious.

"I love you too." The words slip out before I can even think on them. I *know* I'm way more emotional than I should be right now. I'm stuck halfway between the person I really am and the character I promised to play.

I already know I'm freaking out, somewhere deep inside myself. Those aren't words I should even be *pretending* to say. But the emotion behind them feels so real that I can't help letting them out.

And now, oh *god*, I'm crying. What the hell is going on with my brain?

Luke kisses me again. He blinks at the tears and reaches up to brush them away with his thumb. "Hey," he murmurs. "Hey... it's okay."

I bury my face in his shoulder and shiver for a second, trying to figure myself out. He strokes my hair, and I feel... good. I take a deep breath, doing my best to stabilize myself.

It was just... really intense roleplay, I remind myself. *You can chill out now.*

But Luke keeps stroking my hair and brushing his lips

over the top of my head, and I'm just not one hundred percent positive on that. Being in his arms like this is so good, I know I don't want to leave.

"You okay, apples?" he mumbles.

The word hits me like a truck. I swallow hard, but force a nod. I don't *feel* okay. But I don't know exactly how to explain what I do feel, and I'm scared that if I open my mouth, I'll beg him to say those words again for real.

Luke holds onto me quietly for a few minutes while I catch my breath. Eventually, I compose myself enough to speak. "That was…" I laugh nervously. "…intense."

I feel him relax against me some at that. Luke tugs me closer and tucks my head beneath his chin. "That wasn't, uh… exactly how I expected things to go," he admits. "But that was good."

My heart feels like it's trying to escape out my throat again, so I just nod and hold onto him more tightly.

I spend a long time awake in his arms, caught between the bliss of being exactly where I want to be and the sudden worry that I want way more than I should.

10

LUKE

I fall asleep mentally kicking myself. I wake up Sunday, and immediately start the mental thrashing all over again.

Who the hell says I love you in a roleplaying scene? I want to bash my head into a wall to cure my embarrassed horror, but Emily's still sleeping all tangled up in my arms, and the last thing I want to do is wake her up—for more reasons than one.

I was mostly controlling that scene between us. As soon as I said those words, she probably felt pressured to do the same, at least in the moment. I want to hope we'll both just chalk it up as a really intense bit of playacting and safely move on, but I can't shake the ominous feeling that I've seriously fucked up in a way that can't be remedied.

Emily nuzzles into my shoulder, and my heart skips a beat. I close my eyes and stifle a groan.

For years, I've prided myself on keeping my characters firmly separate from my everyday life. And for the most part, it's easy—the real me has absolutely *zero* interest in burning down orphanages and stealing candy from babies, so I don't really have to worry that I'm going to accidentally pick up traits from my fictional personas. I always used to wonder what people meant when they talked about 'game bleed'. Archbishop Devlin Carr does not bleed into Luke West, CPA. When the character sheet goes away, I'm always totally me again, and no one else.

I've never played out a romance with someone I was actually *dating*, though. I've sure as hell never slept with someone *in-character*.

There's a dangerous piece of Sebastian clawing at my heart right now, telling me that this is the love of my life, and I can't let her get away. And I know that's a weird and dangerous feeling to entertain—that it's not based on anything *real*—but that doesn't make the stupid feeling go *away*.

I figured bringing Emily to a weekend game was the perfect gamer date. Gamers game, after all—it's what we both enjoy. But maybe I should have picked a less intense game.

Sheep, I think glumly, as I open my eyes and stare down at her gorgeous face and feel my heart *thud-thud* in my chest. *We should have just rolled some dice and stolen each other's sheep.*

Emily sleeps on, blissfully unaware of my cowardly, sheep-thieving thoughts.

I'm a man halfway-possessed though, and I lean down to kiss the tip of her nose before I can stop myself. She shifts and yawns, and smiles sleepily, and I feel another weird, panicked stab in my heart.

Stop that, I think at that little shard of Sebastian. *You stop that right now. I'm in charge here.*

Emily blinks slowly awake—but her eyes are still unfocused, and she cuddles up closer, as though to defy the idea of getting out of bed. "No," she mumbles stubbornly. "Nuh-uh. Skippin' breakfast."

I can't help the laugh that trickles out. "It's not breakfast yet," I tell her. "You're fine."

Emily smiles triumphantly at this revelation. "Good," she mutters. "'Cos you're warm. And I wouldn't have let you go to breakfast either."

It's the most adorable thing I've ever seen.

I love you. The words are already on my lips again, and I barely manage to choke them back.

I said stop it, Sebastian!

Somehow, I manage to rearrange my expression into something less hopelessly love-struck. I kiss my way down to her ear. "There *are* some things we can do without leaving bed," I murmur there. "Warm things."

Emily's smile goes dreamy. "Oh, *yeah*," she agrees, trailing her fingers up my chest. "I'm all for that."

I kiss her mouth, and all of my worries instantly get shunted away into a corner of my mind. I let myself think how perfect she is, how good it makes me feel to hold her. For the first time, we take it slowly, enjoying the lazy feel of each other's bodies. Right here, right now, the woman I'm kind of *fictionally* in love with is happy to be here with me, and it's helpfully reassuring.

As I slide inside her again, I'm enthralled by the rapturous expression on her face. Emily is more than pleased—she's blissed out, if her sighs are any indication. I like that even better.

Emily looks up at me with a soft smile I haven't seen before. "Okay," she mumbles as she kisses me. "I think I like you when you're nice, too."

I know I grin stupidly at that. *God*, she feels good. "I'll still be mean to you whenever you want," I assure her in a murmur. I pause. "As long as it's... afternoonish."

Emily responds to that with something just between a laugh and a gasp, as she lifts her hips to meet me. Soon, she wraps her legs around my waist, and talking turns into satisfied moans on both sides.

She comes around me with a little hitched breath— and I'm not far behind. I'm convinced that there's nothing in the world more satisfying than the feeling of being in bed with this woman on a weekend.

Eventually, we do pry ourselves out of bed and get ready for game. Emily is wearing another fairly normal-looking outfit that screams *sweet and innocent*, and I'm briefly puzzled. I *know* she brought that giant makeup kit for a reason.

"I thought I'd get to see a different side of Delilah today," I observe, with an arched eyebrow.

Emily leans up to kiss me lightly on the lips. "Later," she promises. "Stop being impatient. Now stay still so I can give you your resting villain face."

After she's painted another sneer onto my lips, I snatch her around the waist and drag her closer. "Hm," I murmur into her ear. "Should I assume last night *really* happened in-game?"

Emily goes pink with embarrassment. "Um... probably," she admits in a small voice.

"*Probably?*" I ask in amusement. "That's a pretty big probably. I guarantee it'll affect the way I treat you today."

Emily presses her lips together, still obviously flushed. "Mm... *yes,*" she admits. "I meant yes."

"Well then, Delilah," I murmur, slipping halfway into character. "Don't worry about any last words. If someone tries to hurt you today, I guarantee they'll die screaming." I pause. "Call it a *personal* guarantee."

Emily hesitates at that. Her brow knits worriedly.

"...it's okay if they deserve it, isn't it?" I say with a grin.

Emily sighs heavily. For a second, it looks like she might respond—but she closes her mouth and shakes her head.

"Good girl," I say. I lean down and kiss her again, and we head out to join the others.

EMILY

I'm a hot mess.

I know I look like I'm cool as a cucumber—but that's mostly because makeup is my war paint, and I'm wearing just enough of it to keep a poker face. Underneath, I'm a seething cauldron of fucked-up emotion, and I honestly don't know what to do about it.

Last night was *good.* This morning was... *also* good. I've never felt so deeply satisfied by casual morning sex before. All those little kisses and caresses turned me to putty, and that's just not normal for me. I prefer my sex just a little rough—or at least, I *did.* I still do? Another hard, hair-pulling fuck against the wall still sounds *amazing.* But I also desperately want to wake up next to Luke again so he can kiss my nose and sigh into my ear.

Luke. He's the thing that's confusing my normal villainous lusts. Every time I think of him, I get a soft, fuzzy feeling that makes me want to go bury myself in his arms again. For the last little bit, he's generously tightened all my loose screws *and* showered me with honest affection. Apparently, I can do nice guys just fine, as long as they don't mind *pretending* to be jerks on occasion.

Is that just another kink? Like, maybe some people like elf ears, and some people like blindfolds, and I just... need pretend bad boys.

When you put it that way, it sounds way healthier than it probably is, I think to myself ruefully.

But the real kicker—the really awful, *weird* part—is that right after we had that fantastic, lazy, sweet-as-sugar sex... he said that thing. The part about *I won't let anyone hurt you,* or something.

And I suddenly felt so fucking wretched I could *cry*.

It hit me basically out of nowhere. Bang, boom. Two seconds prior, if you'd asked me whether I was excited to tear out this man's heart and make him eat it, I'd have told you *hell yes—and he'll thank me for it, too*. But the sheer awfulness of what Corinna and I cooked up slaps me in the face, and in the space of those two seconds, I no longer want to do it. I feel like a horrible, trashy human being for ever wanting to hurt this man.

I *know* he'll enjoy me hurting him. I never said it was *rational*, god damn it.

I'm beginning to think I've been playing Delilah too long. It makes sense for *her* to be upset about this. There's nothing even slightly gleeful about what Delilah has to do today. In fact... in fact, from her perspective, this is all horrifically awful.

Great, I think glumly, as we all start up our first scene for the day. *Either I'm Emily who's dangerously in love with a guy she basically just met, or else I'm Delilah who just wants to run home and cry. Neither one of my weird personalities is super happy right now.*

As we settle into a side room for our little morning war meeting, Luke ends up on my side of the group, instead of next to his supposed allies. He has his hand subtly pressed against my lower back, like he's trying to lend me some support. He's still a bitter asshole, but there's just no hiding the way he stays so close to me, or the way he sometimes side glances me to check if I'm okay.

His brother Daniel—*Elisha*, I remind myself—gives us both a very weird look. I know exactly what he's thinking, and I hate myself just a little bit more every time he glances my way.

I know! I want to scream. *I know it's a bad idea, and I did it anyway, okay?*

"As we suspected—this is not the first time that the black gate has come loose," Silhouette whispers. She's settled herself at the center of the group, so we can all just barely hear her if we lean in to listen. "There is a ritual to seal it closed once more, but it requires one of each of us. Some of the things it asks... they will not be very pleasant."

"What things?" Reckless asks warily.

"I have not been able to discover them all," Silhouette tells him softly. "I tried to find ghosts to tell me of the last ritual, but the gate has made them scarce. I had to dive into unconscious ancestral memories instead. They are... less reliable." She shakes her head tiredly. "I know that the Ghostspeaker must offer up their primary spirit. I mean... *my* primary spirit."

That gets everyone's attention. Even Luke's character hisses in his breath. "Your mother?" he asks sharply. "You have to give up your mother's ghost?"

Silhouette looks down in silence. Her lack of reply says more than one of her whispered answers would do.

Luke's fingers twitch at my back. "Anyone else know what they're supposed to be doing for this ritual?" he asks, with a brand new edge to his voice.

Reckless shrugs carefully. "I'm a Hollow," he says. "None of my magic belongs to me in the first place. As far as I can tell, I just have to bind the other parts of the ritual together." He smiles crookedly. "I'm your magical glue, basically."

"Do you know what you must do, Sebastian?" Silhouette asks quietly.

Luke shakes his head slowly. "Just so happens, someone *burned* most of my faction's research on the subject a few years back. Nasty blood magic has no place in this world, you know." He doesn't look at me or Elisha, but I wince. We all know that the Throne had a hand in that little incident.

"And what about the Throne?" Reckless asks. His eyes fix directly on me, and I look away quickly before I can meet his gaze by accident.

Elisha hesitates. I cut in before he can answer. "We'll know when the time comes," I say. "Don't worry about us."

Reckless raises an openly-skeptical eyebrow. Silhouette frowns. "The rest of us are not used to relying on faith," she whispers. "I do not like the idea of *hoping* that you will have what is necessary in order to fulfill your part."

I'm saved, thankfully, from having to answer this—because Corinna hurries in and taps me on the shoulder, and whispers something in my ear.

I cough purposely on my words. I blink a few times.

Luke glances at me, but I sidestep his touch for the first time this morning. "I... I have some research I can look into," I say hoarsely. "I'll let you know if I can find anything."

Luke grabs my arm as I turn to flee the room, but Corinna shakes her head at him. "Emily promised to do my makeup," she winks. "We're out of character for just a bit."

Daniel puts a hand on Luke's shoulder. "Just assume I've stopped you from leaving, then," he says wryly. "We can argue about it if you want."

Corinna heads upstairs with me, and she's got an obvious spring in her step. "I wonder if Luke's starting to suspect," she mutters at me. "Do you think he knows?"

My stomach churns. I've spent the last two weeks excitedly helping Corinna build up to this plot—and now I just feel gutted by it. I don't know how to admit how unreasonably upset I am about it. It's a good plot. She put a lot of work into it, especially given how last-minute this was.

Ugh, I feel like an *awful* player.

I close the door behind us as we head into the room I share with Luke. Corinna looks at me and pauses, knitting her brow. "Are you all right?" she asks.

I'm horrified to realize that my lip is quivering.

"I'm..." I take a shaky breath. "I'm sorry. I'm so sorry. I'm... really upset. I don't even really know why. It just hit me out of the blue." Tears start trickling down my face, and I wipe at them in alarm.

Corinna helps me sit down on the bed. She's surprisingly calm and level-headed, given that I've just started having a nervous breakdown in front of her. "Okay," she says carefully. "Breathe. Have you had enough to eat and drink today? Did you get enough sleep?"

I nod miserably. I want to explain that I *kind of* know why I'm freaking out, but my voice won't work.

"Are you maybe on your period?" Corinna asks a bit hopefully. Period crazy is relatively easy to solve, after all. "I could get you some painkillers, or some chocolate."

I shake my head at that one, though it gets a little laugh from me. "I... ugh, I'm sorry," I mumble. "I *know* why I'm like this. I just don't want to tell you." I take in a deep, shuddering breath. "I'm upset about the plot. I swear, I was all for it up until like... an hour ago. Then it kind of hit me all at once, and it just... *got* to me."

Corinna blinks at that. She lets out a huge, relieved breath. "Oh, man," she says. "Oh, that's *easy*. I was terrified you were going to say I accidentally dug up some of your real-life trauma or something." She presses a hand to her chest. "Holy crap. Okay." She shakes her head. "No problem, sweetheart. None at all. Let's change the plot."

I stare at her, dumbfounded. "What... just like that?" I ask hoarsely.

Corinna raises both eyebrows at me. "You're so upset you're *crying,*" she tells me. "You really think I'm going to tell you to go downstairs and do something that makes you so unhappy? I mean... even if you *weren't* technically paying me to be here, that'd be awful of me."

I press my lips together. "You were really excited to do

this," I say in a small voice. I'm already feeling better at how instantly she offered up the possibility, though. A second ago, I was resigned to ending this weekend on a really low, wretched note. Now... well, I'm still *embarrassed*, but I also feel like I can breathe normally for the first time since Luke said those words to me and triggered this weird freak-out.

Corinna smiles sympathetically. "I'm excited to give my players what they *want*," she corrects me. "If you don't want it, it's not fun." She slides an arm gingerly around my shoulders, and I relax with a relieved sigh. "Now, we've got a little bit of time up here to brainstorm. What's got you so upset about the plot? Let's start there, so we can figure out how to change it."

I swallow and try to think. Part of me knows what's got me upset, but it's still so hard to admit it out loud, even with the gamemaster earnestly asking me to tell her.

"I..." I look down at my hands. "I really want a happy ending," I whisper.

Corinna's smile turns oddly understanding. "Don't we all," she says softly.

"That's not really what this game is about though, is it?" I ask quietly. "Everyone here seems super willing to die and kill each other and get tortured. I knew it was like this when I agreed to come. I... I even *thought* I was really into the idea. But I'm really messed up about it now. And I *know* a happy ending isn't what anyone *else* here wants."

Corinna squeezes my shoulder. "Hey," she says. "It's okay to be wrong about what you can handle—*especially* in a game like this. I'm just glad you told me, instead of just running ahead with everything like it was okay."

I bite my lip. "I still don't want to mess up anyone else's good time," I admit.

Corinna scoffs. "What kind of gamemaster do you think I am?" she asks. "I've been doing this for like a decade now. I can come up with something to please my sadists *and* my masochists *and* my happy ending people." She nudges me with her elbow. "I'm already getting ideas."

I cross my arms over my chest with a long breath and give a careful nod.

"I'll tell you what," Corinna says. "I still want to see what the other players come up with when you drop this bombshell. But if *they* don't come up with a creative way to handle it, I triple-pinky-promise you, I'll step in and fix it myself. Okay? One way or another, *your* character will have a happy ending. She'll head off into the sunset with her evil boy-toy and live, uh. *Relatively* happily-ever-after." Corinna searches my face for signs that I'm feeling better. "Does that help?"

I nod and sniffle and rub at my eyes again. "Yeah," I mumble. "God. That really helps."

Corinna beams at that. "All right. We've got a deal. You just enjoy tearing Luke's heart out of his chest, and then I promise I'll fix it right back up again, okay?"

I give a watery grin at that. Somehow, that *does* sound better.

"I honestly don't know why it matters so much to me," I admit. "It's just a game. None of this is real. I mean... I'll be back at work tomorrow."

Corinna rolls her eyes. "Don't put yourself down over this," she says. "You ever seen a movie that made you cry? Read a book that upset you?"

I nod, very slowly.

"Well this is even *more* personal than that," Corinna tells me. "You're the one the story is *happening* to, sweetheart. You're not just watching it on a screen. You've got people yelling at you and touching you and treating you like you're someone else. It's gonna get to you. We even have a word for it—we call it *bleed*. You start getting into the story and identifying with your character so much that you get emotional about it."

I blink a few times at that. Is that what I'm doing? *Jesus,* I think. *No wonder I'm a mess. Delilah's life is a weird-ass soap opera, and I'm totally buying into it.*

Another pin clicks into place then, and I close my eyes and sigh.

I'm not in love with Luke—I'm playing a *character* who's in love with his *character*. It's just bleeding over into me because everything is so intense, and I can't tell what emotions belong to which part of me anymore.

"Hey," I ask softly, opening my eyes again. "Um." I rub my hands together nervously. "How do I get *rid* of bleed?"

Corinna considers that for a long moment. "I guess that depends," she says. "What part of it do you want to get rid of? I mean, I'm gonna be honest... most people come here *for* the bleed. It's kind of like a safe way to blow off steam. As long as we fix your ending, you should get a nice little hit of catharsis at the end, right?"

I wince. "Well... more like..." I try to find a way to phrase my response that *won't* make things super uncomfortable for her with Luke. "Say I'm playing someone's best friend. And then I start feeling like I'm going to miss them *really hard* once I go back to real life."

Corinna purses her lips. "Well... do you *want* a new

best friend?" she asks. "It wouldn't be the first time one of these relationships turned into something permanent."

I knit my brow at that. I'm about to say *yeah, but I can't just decide to fall in love with someone because of a make-believe years-long love story*—but we're not talking about that. I clear my throat uncomfortably. "It's not *real*, though," I point out carefully. "We might totally hate each other in real life. There's no way I'd even know."

Corinna shrugs and pushes up to her feet. "Emotions are seriously weird stuff," she advises me. "If it's a nice feeling and a nice relationship, I don't know if I'd assume it's doomed to mess me up. But if you're super worried about it, then distance and routine will do the trick. Just go home, break off contact, and be yourself *really hard* for a few days."

I almost wince at that. *Break off contact.* Even the hint of the idea makes me uncomfortable. I don't *want* to break off contact with Luke. I mean, I don't know if I should be falling in *love* with him this quick, but I do still feel like we've got a good thing started.

I shake my head and rub at my face. *Later,* I promise myself. *I don't have to decide on this now. I've got grisly makeup to do, and a plot to break wide open.*

"All right," I say, with a little more determination in my voice. "What do you say we turn you into a hideous demon?"

Corinna beams at me with genuine pleasure. "I thought you'd never ask," she says.

11

LUKE

*I*t's hard keeping my mind on the scene at hand, instead of wondering what kind of makeup Emily is doing upstairs. Still, it's in-character for me to be distracted right now, so it's not the worst thing in the world.

"You should have stayed away from her," Daniel says quietly. His voice drags me back to the present, and I frown for a second before I remember he's playing Elisha-the-Holy-Asshole.

"You should know better than to tell me what I *shouldn't* do," I tell him, with a harsh smile. "Feeling jealous, Favored Son?"

Daniel shakes his head disapprovingly at me. "Every time I convince myself you're just tragically misguided," he says, "you remind me how much you enjoy what you are." He looks away. "You deserve whatever pain you receive today. If you're still capable of feeling pain, that is."

My jaw tightens at that. Our character backgrounds

were pretty clear on how badly our brotherly relationship has deteriorated by now. But there's a soft touch on my sleeve, and I snap my gaze back to see Silhouette standing quietly at my side.

"I must speak with you, Sebastian," she says quietly. "Now."

I jerk my arm away from her.

"Someday," I whisper to Daniel, "you're going to get what *you* deserve."

Daniel gives me a bemused smile, and I know he's broken character in spite of himself. *Am I going to die again?* his face implies. He clears his throat with effort and tries to force the smile down. "I have faith that you are right, Sebastian," he says.

I turn on my heel and stalk for the hallway. Silhouette follows quietly behind me.

"What is it?" I demand, as soon as we're outside. "What's so god-damned important?"

Silhouette regards me with absolute calm. "Were you aware that the Throne has brought blood magic with them?" she asks me.

That brings me up short. I blink a few times. "What?" I manage. "No. Elisha's a petty, vindictive piece of shit—but of all people, I *know* how much he hates blood magic."

Silhouette shakes her head very slowly. "It is not Elisha," she says softly.

It takes a second for that to sink in.

"...I don't know where you got your information from," I say. "But that's just stupid. Delilah isn't carrying any blood magic on her."

Silhouette frowns carefully. "Have you checked?" she asks me.

I press my lips together. "Why would I check?" I snap. "That's not exactly the first thing that comes to mind when I run into a Throne!"

Out-of-character, I'm *positive* that Silhouette is right, and I've just stumbled on the big, important thread that makes up Emily's plot. But in-character, I'm head-over-heels in love and desperate not to believe the worst.

"Perhaps it *should* be something you consider from now on," Silhouette says quietly. "It has occurred to me, Sebastian... we all *assumed* that the Throne burned the research that they found. But that is not a safe assumption, is it? It is human to keep power for oneself, no matter the origin. And while the Throne Itself may not be human... Its servants certainly are."

I grab her by the shoulders. "You're. Wrong," I grit out. "You don't even have an inkling just *how* fucking wrong you are. Delilah would never touch blood magic."

Silhouette's eyes flicker past my shoulder and settle onto something there. She sighs heavily.

I have a feeling I know the general nature of what I'll see when I turn around. But when I do, the reality of it slams into my chest like a semi-truck.

Emily is standing behind us, leaning heavily against the wall. Her face is unnaturally pale—there are black circles under her eyes and hollow places in her cheeks. Blood trickles from her eyes, her nose, her mouth. She looks like a walking plague victim.

"What the hell?" I whisper.

Emily closes her eyes. "I'm so sorry, Seb," she says in a trembling voice. "I don't want to do this."

She's done a fantastically *awful* job on her makeup. I have to work to suppress the real flutter of fear in my chest, looking at her like that. It's my own natural instinct to rush toward her, to catch Emily as she wavers on her feet.

I look around in a swelling panic, like I'm searching for someone to help her. But it occurs to me a second later that *I'm* that person. I start looking for Corinna instead, knowing that I need a gamemaster for this.

Corinna is standing a short ways back from Emily with a wide, shit-eating grin on her face. It's even more disturbing than it should be, since Corinna's actually had her face painted with hideous gore, like the description she gave of the bloody old woman in front of the ranch.

"Uh," I say. "Are you *here*, Cor? Like... should I be reacting to you like you're really standing there, all covered in blood?"

Corinna shakes her head with a grin. "Not yet," she tells me. "But soon." Corinna crosses her arms. "Why? Did you *need* something, Luke?"

I narrow my eyes at her. "What the ever-loving hell is wrong with Delilah? And *yes*, I'm checking for blood magic!"

Corinna smiles innocently. "Delilah is carrying a powerful blood magic artifact," she tells me. "She's probably been carrying it for a while now, based on the damage it's caused to her body. The artifact is deeply connected to her, and it's not playing nice with her magic. She's doing really badly right *now,* but if you got rid of whatever she's carrying, she'd probably recover after a few days."

I look back at Emily. "Where's the item?" I ask her. "I'm *definitely* honing in on it using blood magic."

Emily presses her lips together. They look like they're cracked and bleeding. *Damn,* that makeup job is unsettling. She pulls a wooden prop knife from her pocket and presses it into my hands. I recognize it from one of her previous cosplays; it's painted to look real, and it's got a better, more realistic heft to it than a latex version would.

I snatch the knife from her with renewed fury and grab her by the arm. "What is this?" I hiss. "What have you *done*, Dee?"

Emily shakes her head at me blankly. Her lips tremble, and her eyes grow wet with tears. Those tears worry me at first—but since they turned on like a light switch, I'm fairly sure they're part of Emily's act, and not coming from Emily herself.

"I didn't choose this," she chokes out. "It chose *me*."

"Let her go, Sebastian." Daniel's voice sounds from behind me. "You don't know what's going on."

I whirl around to see Daniel standing in the doorway of the room that me and Silhouette exited earlier, though I keep one hand on Emily. "Maybe if someone else *knows* what's going on, then they should fucking *tell* me!" I demand in a hiss.

Daniel sighs heavily. "Delilah said that *she* was going to tell you," he says. "She insisted."

I look back at Emily. Tears have left track marks in the fake blood on her face now.

"I can't," she whispers miserably. "I thought I could... but I can't."

Daniel shakes his head. "Then *I* will." He straightens to his full, very impressive height. "The Throne found this knife among a stash of materials on blood magic. We kept it for study, to try and determine its purpose—so that we could fight things like this in the future, if need be." He pauses wearily. "But the research that came with it suggested that this artifact is part of an ancient compact between our factions. Its name is *Gevurah*. Severity. When the black gate threatens, *Gevurah* chooses a slayer to perform a sacrifice, as part of the ritual... and it also chooses a lamb."

Corinna smiles at me again from over Emily's shoulder. The smile shows the fake blood on her teeth. "The knife knows you, Sebastian," she tells me, with a low, dark chuckle. "You're connected to it too."

I drop the knife like it's burned me. It clatters to the floor.

"No," I whisper. "*Hell* no."

Emily stares at me. She doesn't seem to know how to react.

"Why?" I beg her. "Why... why would you..." I suck in a shuddering breath. "You knew this the whole time, and you *still*..." I'm unreasonably proud of my ability to force out a few tears on the spot. "Are you *enjoying* this? Did you just want to hurt me on your way out?"

Emily's lip trembles. Her breath hitches. She throws herself into my arms and presses her face against my chest. "I'm sorry. I'm *sorry*. I..." Her fingers twist helplessly in my shirt. "I thought it would be easier if... if I at least knew that you *cared*." Her voice catches wretchedly on the words. "I was wrong." The last sentence is barely a whisper. It's so well-done that it jabs at my heart in a very real way.

Daniel moves to grab the knife—but I whirl on him,

pressing my foot down overtop it. "You piece of shit," I grit out. "You brought her here. You *knew* what was going on, and you dragged her here to shove her at me like some kind of animal going to slaughter!"

Daniel takes a step back, at least somewhat unnerved by the violent expression on my face. "The black gate *must* be closed," he says slowly. "This isn't how any of us want to do it either, Sebastian. But if that gate cracks open, even just a little bit, *far* more people will suffer and die than just Delilah."

I choke on a furious, ironic laugh. "*One for a thousand*," I manage. "From *you*, Elisha?" I shake my head incredulously. "Just so I know—how does *that* hypocrisy taste?"

A few of the other players have started huddling in the doorway just behind Elisha, straining to see what's going on. Corinna steps forward and claps her hands. "This is a great scene," she says. "But it's getting a little crowded in the hallway. Can we move it back into a bigger room, just for the sake of everyone having space to breathe?"

I reach down to grab the knife again, so we can side-step back into the bigger room. I've still got Emily by the arm. She's doing a great job of looking miserable and subdued—honestly, I'm a *little* worried about it.

"Hey," I murmur. "This is *awful*. I love every second of it." I glance down toward her as we walk, and pause just outside of the side room. "Just so I know, though... do you *want* me to sacrifice your little Throne and spend the rest of my days in self-loathing misery?"

Emily looks faintly surprised by the question. "Um..."

She flushes and looks down. "Would you be upset if I said *no?*"

I blink. "Why would I be upset?" I ask. "It's your character. You get a say too."

Emily smiles suddenly at that. Before I know exactly what's going on, she's thrown her arms around my neck and leaned up onto her tiptoes to give me a kiss. "That's very nice of you," she mumbles at me. She lowers herself to the ground again shyly. "I don't think I like unhappy endings. I hope that's not a dealbreaker."

I'm still blinking away the surprise of that kiss. It takes me a second to catch up to what she's said. "A deal-breaker?" I ask.

"Um. Relationship-wise?" Emily looks embarrassed. "I don't know. You just... really seem to like the edgy stuff. I wouldn't want to be your personal buzzkill all the time."

I laugh a little at that and pull her into a hug. "You are *far* from killing my buzz," I tell her. "I'm having fun."

Emily relaxes into my arms with a sigh. I run my fingers absently through her hair. "All right," I murmur. "Let's go screw up a sacrifice, shall we?"

Emily shoots me a wry smile at that. "You are... basically the *best*," she tells me. "Just so you know."

That smile digs down into my chest like every other one today and steals my breath away. I don't even try to stop it this time.

EMILY

The warm, fuzzy feeling I get when Luke asks me what I want him to do with my character is similar to the one I got when he kissed my nose this morning. But this time, I *know* it's a hundred percent my own warm fuzzies and not Delilah's.

I trust him. The realization builds very slowly within me as we take up our places to begin the scene again. Every time I've been vulnerable or uncertain or upset around this man, he's done his best to make it better. That's not a quality Sebastian possesses—it's all Luke. And I can't remember the last time I felt that way around a man I was dating.

Well. Actually, I *can* remember. The answer is never. I didn't even realize guys this decent and patient and sweet actually existed—though I guess I should have *assumed* that they did, based on Liv and Finn's sugary-sweet relationship.

The fact that Luke's gone out of his way to ask me what I want to do banishes any last vestiges of worry from my mind. I'm actually feeling excited to play out the rest of this plotline again, in all its hideous, miserable glory.

Luke slides the knife back under his shoe and grabs my arm again. Silhouette and the other players crowd in, but this time there's a lot more space to spread out. Reckless has taken instant notice, in particular—he's standing very near to Luke, watching him with a sharp-edged ferocity. If things go downhill between Luke and Elisha, I have no doubts that Reckless will decide to take advantage of the situation to remove his enemy.

Daniel clears his throat sheepishly. "I don't remember where we were," he admits.

"Uh... *how does hypocrisy taste?*" I volunteer.

Daniel beams at me. "Right," he says. "Thanks." He does his best to arrange his features into a scowl, but it doesn't look terribly convincing on him. "Don't talk to *me* about hypocrisy!" he growls at Luke. "How many years have you spent insisting that this sort of thing is necessary? How many people have you killed who had others that cared about them? Now that it's someone *you* care about—someone who's *volunteering*, no less—suddenly, you can't bring yourself to do it?"

"I'm not going to *murder* the woman I love!" Luke bursts out violently. The sheer vitriol in his voice takes the whole room aback for just a second. It's weird to remember that we can yell and scream here without drawing the wrong attention—it's the whole point of having an entire ranch to ourselves.

Luke has shoved me back behind him—Sebastian is now implicitly protecting me from Elisha, my actual ally. It's a weird switcheroo of a scenario.

"You think I like doing this?" Luke yells hoarsely. "You think I *enjoy* it?" He snatches up *Gevurah* in his hand again, holding it tightly by the blade. If it was a real knife, it would be cutting into his palm by now, and everyone knows it. "I didn't *choose* this magic! I wasn't some goddamn psychopath who went and tracked it down!"

His breathing is harsh. He's got the whole room staring at him, enthralled. It's an emotional monologue, and he's carrying it off well.

"Every time," Luke rasps, "you hand me the goddamn knife and look away. *All* of you." I can feel his hand trembling on my arm. "You justify it to yourselves by pretending I'm some evil, heartless son of a bitch, so you don't have to think about the blood that *you* keep putting on my hands."

Luke looks around at the other players as he speaks. Some of them meet his eyes calmly. Others glance uncomfortably at the floor. Silhouette simply looks at him as though she's trying to fit this new aspect into her understanding of him.

Reckless has a strange expression on his face—a dawning, horrified guilt that he can't quite hide.

Luke throws the knife roughly at Elisha's feet. "I'm not doing it this time," he spits. "Not *this* time. You want to spill some blood for the greater good, you go ahead and do it yourself, you fucking saint. You'll have to kill me first—but I'm sure *that* blood doesn't bother you either."

Daniel shakes his head slowly. "I can't," he says softly. "I can't be the slayer—just like I can't be the lamb. I would have taken her place otherwise. You have to believe that." He looks past Luke toward me. "Delilah knows that, Sebastian. That's why she volunteered to come here with me."

Luke swallows hard. He turns to look at me. "Is that what you want, Dee?" he asks, in a trembling voice. He takes my face in his hands, forcing me to look up at him. His red eyes are full of tears, and it's *impressive*. "You really want to die? You really want me to... to *kill* you?"

I really can't answer him for a second. Delilah doesn't know what she wants. From an outside perspective, it's easy to see how thoroughly she's been brainwashed by her faction. She can't imagine letting down the people who taught her everything she knows. But *obviously*, she doesn't want to die. This whole thing terrifies her completely, and there's no way to change that.

"Yeah," Luke says softly. "I thought not."

"She didn't tell you no," Daniel observes in a hard voice.

Luke turns on him again. "She didn't tell me *yes*," he hisses.

Corinna steps between them, holding up a hand. "Boys," she says with a smirk. "Pause for a second, please. I need to describe a change in the scene." She straightens up and looks around at the gathered players. "The earth trembles. Somewhere deep beneath your feet, a crack begins to open in the gate. You feel a cold, hideous darkness clawing at your souls. Distant moans of agony arise in the air around you."

She smiles. "I appear in the room, exactly as you see me. It's easy now for all of you to recognize a demon when you see one. I have no body, and I cannot be dispelled by normal means." She claps her hands again once. "Time in! As you were!"

Daniel staggers back instantly from Corinna, fumbling for the notecard that represents his Throne talisman. He presents it toward the gamemaster, but she laughs contemptuously at it this time.

"Favored Son," Corinna says, with a rictus grin. "We are too strong for your little toy now. All you have left is your faith... and how well does that serve you?" She reaches up to brush a hand along Daniel's jaw, and he looks at her in horror. "We knew when we first saw you that you were weak," she sneers. "True faith needs no *talismans*."

Daniel jerks back from her quickly, swallowing. He looks toward Luke with a wild fear in his eyes. "We can't let this thing walk free," he manages hoarsely.

Silhouette looks toward Corinna calmly. "Those who are willing should begin the ritual," she says in her soft voice. "We have no time for the rest. We must hope that what we have is sufficient."

Corinna whirls on her with a hiss. "We will take what you love and tear it to *pieces*, Ghostspeaker," she growls.

Silhouette stays very still. She trembles for a moment, but doesn't look away. Eventually, Corinna stalks past her toward Reckless.

"You are nothing but a vessel for power, Hollow," Corinna murmurs to him. "We can give you power. *So* much power. Enough to protect you against the ones who have hurt you so much. Enough to make sure they never hurt *anyone* again."

Reckless closes his eyes and presses his hands to his forehead. The gamemaster leans in toward him. "Power has no agenda, Hollow," she whispers. "What we give you, you can use as you like. Whatever you may think of us, you can turn our power to good."

Reckless opens his eyes with a shuddering breath. He looks past Corinna toward Luke. "I don't know what's good anymore," he says softly. "I can't be trusted with that."

Corinna hisses again, pretending frustration. She takes long, cat-like strides back toward Luke and me, and her bloody smile widens again. "*Sanguinist,*" she purrs. "One can be more valuable than even a thousand. You understand now, don't you? The Throne believes only in black and white. But you have seen their ugly shades of gray. They lie to you. They lie *about* you. They lie about *us.*"

Luke shoves me warily behind him again. "Don't try and fuck with my head," he growls. "The Throne is full of hypocrites. So what else is new? At least they're *capable* of hypocrisy. You're just a mindless spirit with a cartoon villain agenda."

Corinna laughs. "But you will not slay the lamb," she says, with obvious pleasure.

Luke narrows his eyes at Corinna. He brings up the out-of-character sign. "This knife," he says slowly. "It wants Delilah's *blood*, right?"

Corinna inclines her head in agreement. Her eyes sparkle, as though she already knows what he's going to say.

Luke smiles. "So, let's say I... *switched* her blood with someone else's," he offers. "Would that be sufficient to create a brand new lamb?"

Corinna spreads her hands. "In theory... sure," she agrees. "Though I'm sure the process of switching blood with someone else wholesale would be horrifically painful."

Luke scoffs. "I don't save lives very often," he says. "People ought to be glad I'm doing it at all, instead of complaining about the *how*." He glances back toward me. "I could switch my blood with Delilah's. There's a certain amount of satisfying *fuck you* involved, killing myself to bind a demon."

My mouth drops open. "What—*you?*" I say. "Are you doing the redemption arc thing, Luke?"

I'm just trying to work my brain through the implications of this and whether I'm happy with that sort of ending... but Luke frowns. "Holy hell, you're right," he says. "What am I doing? I'm playing a selfish *bastard*." He turns toward the rest of the room and raises his voice. "Who here wants me to brutally murder them to save my girlfriend's life?"

I should not be at *all* surprised by now at how many hands leap into the air without hesitation.

Luke raises an eyebrow at Silhouette, who's eagerly waving her hand around like a teacher's pet at the front of the class. "Oh, come on," he tells her. "I don't have enough of a grudge against you."

Silhouette pouts. "But I'd get to haunt you *forever* afterward," she says.

Reckless snaps his fingers to draw attention to himself. "Hey!" he says. "We've got a score to settle. And I'm feeling just guilty enough I'd probably *let* you do it."

Luke smiles slowly at that. "No," he says. "No, I think I'm going to use that some other way. Hold that thought for a second." He turns to face Daniel, who—smiling ruefully—has his hand lightly raised in front of him.

"Third time's the charm?" Daniel suggests with a laugh.

Luke shrugs. "It kind of fits. I like it."

Daniel nods somberly. "I hate this character, Luke," he says. "He's a sanctimonious shithead. Put him out of his misery."

Luke reaches out to shake his brother's hand. "Done and done," he declares. "Fratricide it shall be."

"Oh my *god*," I manage. "You guys are so weird."

Luke grins back at me. "Come on," he says. "You've gotta admit, there's a certain poetry to it."

I sigh. "There really is. It ties everything up with a neat little bow. I mean—a *horrible* little bow."

Luke lets go of Daniel's hand and settles back onto his heels. "Time in, Corinna," he says. "Three—two—one."

Corinna's face relaxes back into that triumphant smirk as she goes back into character. "We thought not," she sneers. "We thank you for your forbearance, Sanguinist."

Luke sets his jaw. He turns his head to look toward Daniel... then toward Reckless. Slowly, he straightens his spine.

"Hold my brother down," he tells Reckless in a low, ominous tone. "And I'll forget your secrets forever."

Reckless widens his eyes. He glances sharply over at Daniel, who knits his brow in feigned confusion.

Slowly, comprehension begins to dawn on Daniel's face. He takes a step back. "You're insane," he whispers. "You can't *do* this, Sebastian."

"Can't I?" Luke mocks him. "I thought you said you'd take her place if you could, *Elisha.*"

Corinna steps back, watching the two of them with a hungry, curious look in her eyes.

Daniel lunges for the knife on the floor between them. Reckless hesitates for only one more second... but an instant later, he grabs at Daniel, hauling him back. Luke snatches up *Gevurah* with a horrible laugh and pretends to slash Daniel across the arm.

I realize belatedly that I'm still playing Delilah, watching this unfold in front of me. *What do I do?* I think. *I'm watching the man I love attack my best friend.*

"Seb," I manage. "What... what are you doing?"

Luke narrows his eyes at me. "I'm making a choice," he says. "Don't worry, Dee. I won't make you play a part in it. I've got years more practice being a horrible person than you do." He whirls on me, tearing off his tie and shoving it into my mouth. I blink and try to jerk back, but he holds it in place. "Bite down on this and try not to swallow your tongue or anything. I don't know how bad this is going to be."

I make a muffled noise around his tie as he presses the wooden knife against my arm and slices it downward.

"I start switching their blood," he informs Corinna pleasantly.

Daniel screams and thrashes. Reckless holds him down, looking vaguely nauseous.

I let my knees give out and do my best to follow suit. Luke catches me as I pitch forward, letting me carefully down to the floor.

He brushes his fingers along my cheek and smiles. "I guess I was right," he says. "Someone *will* die screaming today." Luke leans down to kiss my forehead, even while I grasp at his shirt and make vain gestures to try and stop him.

Luke pries my fingers from his shirt and rises back to his feet, with *Gevurah* in hand. I'm barely able to watch from my place on the ground as he heads toward Daniel. Luke pauses to stare down at him for an extended moment. His jaw trembles, and he manages to look uncertain for just a split second.

"Don't... don't do this," Daniel pleads. "*Seb.*"

Luke shakes his head slowly. "I'm just giving you what you've always wanted, Elisha," he says softly. His red eyes glitter. "It's time to be a martyr for your cause."

He brings down the knife. Reckless cringes and looks away, unable to watch.

Daniel goes silent.

Corinna lets out one of those disgusting gurgling cries she's so good at, clutching at her chest.

Nearby, Silhouette snaps a pendant from her neck

and throws it to the floor. She looks down at it and takes a hard breath. "Goodbye, Mother," she says in a calm whisper. Her foot slams down onto the pendant, and Corinna gurgles miserably again.

Luke hurries back toward me, hauling me up from the floor back into his arms. He pries the tie from my mouth and brings his lips down on mine as the various players around us each make their own final, life-altering decisions regarding the ritual.

"What did you do?" I whimper. "What did you *do*?"

"The same thing Elisha asked me to do to *you*," Luke murmurs. "I swear to your stupid Throne, Dee... you're never going back to those bastards again."

I know this is *far* from a finished conversation. There's no way this awful trauma is going to smooth itself over for these two characters in a hurry.

But that just means we'll have *plenty* more to roleplay after this weekend.

I suppress the smile that tries to tug at my lips and let him kiss me, while a bunch of other players send a demon back to hell.

12

———

EMILY

*Y*ou'd think that after all that drama, dinner would be a tense affair. Instead, it's like everyone's somehow let out a giant, relieved breath all at once.

It's easy to tell the game is over—people have started peeling off costume pieces, and everyone's relaxing tiredly back into chairs at the dining table. I'm happily cuddled up beneath Luke's arm again, soaking up the feeling of it with relish. After a weekend of intense role-playing with his (admittedly hot, *very* hot) asshole character, it's actually *nice* just enjoying his normal company.

Daniel's settled in next to us at the table; he's smeared a little fake blood over his character's white dress shirt as a joke, even though the game is over.

"Actually," Luke's brother tells me bemusedly, "I was supposed to be the sacrifice from the beginning. But they split my character into *two* people at the last second. I think Delilah got whatever positive qualities I might have had, along with the death sentence."

I cover my mouth with a gasp. "Oh my god," I say. "I'm so sorry! I didn't realize I'd changed things up for you that much."

Daniel laughs. "It's fine, honestly," he assures me. "I know I play boring lawful good types all the time. It was a good stretch for me to play a bit of a jerk this time. Though... I can't say I'll do it again in a hurry. I definitely prefer being a more straightforward hero."

"I *knew* that shit had to run in the family," Luke mutters next to me.

"What, playing lawful good characters?" I ask him with a snort. "I don't *think* so, Mr. Fratricide."

Luke blinks at me and colors. "Uh," he mumbles. "Never mind."

"I know this is your first time to *this* game," Daniel says to me, grabbing my attention. "But Luke told me you're a gamer already. What else do you play?"

I blink. It hadn't occurred to me that Luke might have already talked to his brother about me before we got to game. I try not to read too much into it. "Oh, I mostly play T&T," I tell him. "I've got a regular group, but I play in Tower Society too, at a lot of the local cons."

Daniel raises his eyebrows. "Oh, neat!" he says. "Maybe I'll see you around! I was hoping to bring my official character into some local games, now that I'm down here permanently."

I straighten in my chair. I can't help it. T&T is my bread and butter, and I'm thrilled to be talking about it after a full weekend out of my normal element. "What kind of character do you play?" I ask Daniel eagerly.

Luke shakes his head ruefully. "Just *guess*," he says.

Daniel rolls his eyes at his brother. "I have a paladin

of Hirtel," he tells me. "I've been playing him for years. He got so high level that I can't really play him now unless there's a special con event—but there's more of those around here than there are in Ontario, for sure."

I actually clap my hands a little and squeal. "Oh man, that's *perfect*," I tell him. "Liv normally plays the paladin in our group at cons, but she's gotten into gamemastering, and now she's always too busy *running* games to play."

Daniel considers that with obvious interest. "Your group?" he asks. "You and Luke?"

I pause at that. *Well.* We did play together once. And it *was* at TowerCon. "I guess so," I tell him, with a hint of a smile. "At least at the con. Me and Luke. And Samson and Jim."

"And Ginny," Luke adds graciously.

Daniel knits his brow at that. "You mean the cute girl you play board games with—"

Luke flushes, looking suddenly horrified. "No," he says. "No, no. Absolutely *not* cute. You're my brother. There's got to be some kind of rule against your brother thinking your friends are *cute*." He reaches up to rub at the bridge of his nose. "Oh my god, someone scrub this profane image from my mind, *please*."

I raise an amused eyebrow at Daniel, and he shrugs. "Not cute," he amends. "We'll say... *nice*. I've met her once or twice. She seems... *nice*."

"Too late," Luke says glumly. "I give up. Let's talk about T&T characters again, please."

We spend the rest of dinner talking about a little of everything—recounting moments from earlier in the weekend, meandering into discussions of T&T games and costuming. Somehow, it already feels like I've known them both forever.

Corinna stops by to give us each a hug and a personal goodbye. Luke passes her a hip flask, and she shoots him a suspicious look. "No alcohol at game," Corinna reminds him.

"It's officially post-game," Luke replies cheerfully. "Have a drink, Cor. You look wiped."

Corinna sighs and takes a swig from the flask. Her shoulders relax, and she passes it back. "I think I'm gonna sleep for a week," she mutters. "Someone call the coroner to check on me if I don't re-emerge from my apartment in the next few days." She shoots me a weary, satisfied smile. "Good first game?"

"*Fantastic* first game," I assure her. "Thank you so much for running."

Corinna's smile goes crooked. "Thanks for the last-day makeup," she replies. "It really made the big scene." She reaches out to squeeze my shoulder. "You're welcome back next year if you want. Though... maybe with more than two weeks' notice, if you don't mind."

"I'm tempted," I admit. "But I think I'll consider it more once I've had a chance to cool down."

People start to file out soon enough. It's not long before there's only a few of us left over, reluctantly considering the time.

"Well," Daniel sighs, as he gathers up his stuff. "I *do* have to go into the shop tomorrow morning. I guess I better start the drive back."

I chew at my lip. Luke's arm tightens around me, and I know what we're both thinking: as soon as we leave, we have to split up again and not see each other for another... how long? Who knows. However long it is, it's definitely not going to be the same waking up in different beds now.

"I, uh..." Luke clears his throat. "I could probably keep the room for one more night," he offers to me. "If we wanted to take off early tomorrow morning instead." He pauses. "*Really* early."

The little rational voice in my head says this is a terrible idea. I'll have to get up two and a half hours earlier than usual. I'll have to wear my clothes from Friday back into work again. I'll have to text Liv and let her know I've changed my plans...

Screw it, I think. *It's worth the misery.*

"Only if you let me pay for the last night," I tell him.

Luke looks too pleased to argue with me. I know he was expecting me to say no. Hell, *I* expected me to say no. But once we see off Daniel in the parking lot, we head inside to sort out another night and stumble back up to our room.

"You, uh... you *did* have a good time?" Luke asks me, as we halfway collapse into bed.

"I did say so," I mumble, as I wiggle my way into his arms. He still smells amazing. *And mine,* my brain suggests, for the very first time.

Luke nods tiredly at that. I can *feel* him chewing things over in his head, struggling to find a diplomatic way to broach the obvious subject. But we're both so exhausted, I feel it's only fair to offer up the blunt approach instead.

"This is really good," I say. "This... *thing.* With us." I pause. "I don't know what to call it. Should we pick something to call it?"

Luke lets out a breath. "Uh... dating?" he offers carefully.

I shake my head with a frown. "More than that," I mumble. *A lot more.* Ugh. "I want to be totally honest. This game screwed with my head. Maybe... in a good way. But still."

He's running his fingers through my hair again, and *god*, I just never want him to stop. "Hm," Luke murmurs. I'm listening carefully for any signs of wariness, but there are none. I still trust him, even though we're talking about far more serious things—*real* things.

I take a deep breath. "I got a little addicted to you this weekend," I tell him. "And I got *really* into character. And... it's hard to separate out all the feelings there. But I've given it a little thought... and I'm not sure I actually *want* to try and separate it out." Luke stills his fingers, and I force myself to jump right in before I can chicken out. "I guess what I'm saying is... I'd like to just fall in love with you and figure out the rest later. Is that totally crazy?"

Luke is quiet for a long moment—and I'm certain now that I've freaked him out. *Shit.* It was the right thing to say, though, I'm positive. I wasn't going to be able to keep this weirdness in forever, and at some point it was probably going to slip out anyway when I least expected it—

"Sure," he mumbles. "Yeah. That sounds... really nice."

What.

Luke turns me over onto my back so he can settle on top of me. His lips brush mine very gently, and I see him looking down at me the same way he's been looking at me all weekend.

"You're not calling me a crazy person," I mumble against him. "I was one hundred percent expecting you to call me a crazy person."

Luke curves his lips upward. "It's been a long weekend," he agrees. "I loved every second of it." He kisses absently along my jaw. "I'm in love with you too. In that weird, half-me kind of way. It's pretty great, isn't it?"

My mouth goes dry. Those words set my heart drumming in my chest, the same way they did the first time. I tighten my arms around him and take in a shuddering breath. "Uh," I manage. I swallow, with difficulty. "Can you... say that again?"

Luke glances up at me and smiles. "It's pretty great, isn't it?" he teases.

I *know* he's messing with me now.

He leans his lips toward my ear. "I love you," he whispers there. "How's that?"

That hot, heady tingle starts up all over my skin again. I'm not even playing a character this time.

"I love you too," I whisper back breathlessly.

It *is* totally crazy. But since neither one of us seems to care, it's definitely the *best* kind of crazy.

EPILOGUE
LUKE

I've spent the last few months waiting for the other shoe to drop.

I mean, sure. My dream woman went on a dream date with me and then decided to just fall in love with me. When you put it that way, how could I possibly complain?

But here we are, months later, and *nothing* terrible has gone wrong. Emily and I still spend every moment together we can manage. Neither of us has any bizarre dealbreakers hiding in our closets. We get along fantastically. Hell, I've stolen her sheep once or twice, and she hasn't even gotten mad at me.

Maybe I've just been playing overly-dramatic games for too long, but I was *sure* something was doomed to go wrong. I wasn't necessarily looking forward to it—just trying to prepare for it.

Instead, I'm just... exceptionally, blissfully happy.

My phone chimes on my way out of work. I glance down at it and grin. It's Friday night, and I'm supposed to meet Emily at the hotel we're staying at for a tiny local convention.

EMILY: Left your keycard at the front desk.

EMILY: Are you wearing a tie?

I snort.

LUKE: I always wear a tie to work.

I get into my car and head for the hotel. By the time I get there, there's another message waiting on my phone.

EMILY: Good. Keep it on.

My eyebrows inch upward. I stop by the front desk and pick up the room key. As I unlock the door to the hotel room, I'm instantly grabbed by the tie and dragged inside.

It takes me a long, stunned moment to realize that my girlfriend is dressed up as a very sexy half-elven fashionista—elf ears, slinky dress, and all.

Emily gives me a sultry smile and shoves me back into a hotel chair. She climbs up into my lap. "I promise," she purrs, "I'm a hundred percent sober. Now—where were we?"

She kisses me, hot and slow, and winds my tie in her hand—and I don't know what I did to deserve this, but I thank Past Me profusely for whatever the hell it was.

"*Wait.*" I force myself to grab her by the shoulders and push her back gently. Emily's mouth drops open, as though I've just insulted her dress stitching. I frown at her. "You're *totally* sober?" I ask suspiciously.

Emily scoffs. "What?" she asks. "Oh my god, *yes.* Why would I lie?"

I shake my head. "Just checking," I tell her. "So... no random marriage proposals tonight?"

Now she's looking *exceptionally* confused. "No," Emily says. "Definitely not."

I sigh heavily. "Damn."

I wasn't planning to spring this for at least a little bit... but how could I possibly pass up this perfect opening?

"I mean," I continue on blandly. "If you're *definitely* not up for any marriage proposals, I guess I can go return the ring."

Emily's face drains of color. It's a good thing she's already sitting in my lap, because I'm pretty sure she might have lost her feet otherwise. "The... ring?" she repeats stiltedly.

I nod sagely. "The one in my suitcase, right next to the door." I slide my hands up the side of her dress and haul her back up against me. *Still no underwear.* God, I'm in heaven. "Don't worry, I'll take it back to the shop first thing tomorrow."

Emily lets out a little whimper into my mouth, and I decide to have some pity. "Oh, *all right,*" I say. "I guess you can see it before I take it back." I slide her off my lap and head over to go rummage a little velvet box from a side pocket in my suitcase.

I get down on one knee in front of my absolutely stunned, absolutely gorgeous, geeky girlfriend, and open up the box to show her the ring.

"It's pretty nice, I think," I observe helpfully. "But since we're not doing marriage proposals tonight—"

"Oh my *god,* you asshole!" Emily bursts out laughing though, and I can see her fighting back little tears in her eyes. She presses at her mouth. "*Yes.*"

My heart speeds up in my chest, but I tilt my head at

her with a frown. "Yes, what?" I ask. "Yes, I should take it back, or yes, you think you'd like to keep it—"

Emily hauls me up by the tie and finally shuts me up.

We pick up right back where we left off... and I've got a feeling it's going to go way better, this time around.

AFTERWORD

I knew as soon as I mentioned Luke's Nordic LARP group that I was going to have to show them on-screen somehow. In the end, I'm pretty pleased with how it all turned out.

Which brings me to the subject of *this* book.

Bleed is a totally natural occurrence in most games. It happens in tabletop games too, but it's especially common in live action roleplaying games. It only makes sense that you'll emotionally invest yourself in a character whose name you actually answer to for a while. That can be great, but it can also do some *seriously* weird things to your head if you're not prepared for it. On the positive side of things, bleed has led to some of the longest, most fantastic friendships of my life. On the less positive side of things, I've seen it lead to lifelong, irrational hatreds between players who stubbornly believe they're unaffected by what happens in-game.

The best way to avoid unpleasant bleed is to make sure you communicate openly and honestly with your gamemaster and your fellow players. In more classical terms, we call this meta-gaming—and for a long time, it was stigmatized as a *bad* thing, because gamemasters assumed that if they gave a player information about the plot that their character didn't know, the player would use it to get an unfair advantage over everyone else.

Here's the thing: if you don't know anything about the plot, you can't express when you're uncomfortable with where it's heading. And if you're the sort of person to take unfair advantage, then you probably shouldn't be at the table in the first place.

In my expert opinion—and I do consider myself an expert, after decades of running games—the best groups run off trust. If you can't trust someone to care about everyone else's fun, then don't let them in the door. If you *do* trust them to care about everyone else's fun, then give them the information they need in order to make the game more fun for everyone.

This doesn't mean I don't like surprises in my games. There's definitely room for surprise in a model like this; as you get to know your fellow players better, you learn how far you can safely push their boundaries, and you don't need to share information so bluntly or ask for their permission quite as much as you once did. I've been running for some of my players for more than a decade now, and they've told me more than once that they love the way I hurt them.

Don't judge me. All authors are just a *little* bit of a sadist to fictional characters.

I guess all of this is just to say: game with people you trust, learn to communicate openly with them, and listen when they tell you they're uncomfortable. Your games will improve significantly... or else you'll quickly learn that you're in the wrong game.

Oh, and also: ask politely before you murder some-one's character. If they're a good sport, they might even suggest a better way to twist the knife.

ABOUT THE AUTHOR

Ivy Collins writes short, geeky romances with a hint of spice. She lives in Montreal, Quebec with her fantastic, prose-inspiring husband and her two cats. When not writing romance, she can be found running D&D or Pathfinder for her local group. She is a veteran gamemaster with more than twenty years of experience.

* * *

Want more short, geeky romances? Keep up with my releases when you sign up for my mailing list.

https://ivycollins.com
info@ivycollins.com

ALSO BY IVY COLLINS

Dating & Dragons

Dating & Dragons

A Wicked Encounter

The Paladin Wears Plaid (Forthcoming)

Standalones

Date My Professor

www.ingramcontent.com/pod-product-compliance
Lightning Source LLC
Chambersburg PA
CBHW021732190726
48288CB00009B/3020